# THREE TO RIDE

## *Nights in Bliss, Colorado 1*

D0862653

## Sophie Oak

**MENAGE AMOUR**

**Siren Publishing, Inc.**
**www.SirenPublishing.com**

**A SIREN PUBLISHING BOOK**
IMPRINT: Ménage Amour

THREE TO RIDE
Copyright © 2011 by Sophie Oak

ISBN-10: 1-61034-036-1
ISBN-13: 978-1-61034-036-6

First Printing: January 2011

Cover design by Jinger Heaston
All cover art and logo copyright © 2011 by Siren Publishing, Inc.

**PUBLISHER**
Siren Publishing, Inc.
www.SirenPublishing.com

# DEDICATION

To Kim. If the universe had asked me what I wanted in a sister, I would never have picked you. Sometimes reality is better than fantasy.

Special thanks to my family for giving me the time to write, to the towns of South Fork and Creede in Colorado for the inspiration, and to my writer buddies, Kris Cook and Shayla Black for always listening when I drone on and on.

# THREE TO RIDE

*Nights in Bliss, Colorado 1*

## SOPHIE OAK

## Prologue

Elizabeth Courtney stared dully out the hospital window. It was a gray day outside. It seemed like it would never stop raining.

"We'll give you protection." The officer had made that promise three times now. He kept looking over her file and saying the same things.

"For how long?" Liz asked, knowing the answer wouldn't be to her liking.

The male officer shifted from foot to foot and scratched at the hair under his black cap. "For as long as you need it."

"I doubt that," she replied. It would be for as long as they had the budget for it, if that. Tommy still had friends on the force. Just because he'd turned out to be a complete psycho freak didn't mean they would desert him. Cops tended to stick together, especially on big-city police forces. Liz had already gotten a phone call from Tommy's old partner threatening her if she didn't drop the case against him. Of course, at the time, her case had been stalking. She could now add arson and attempted murder to the list. God, she thought, still dazed at the last twenty-four hours, how could one date have gone so wrong? Her stomach felt leaden. Her heart started to pound.

"She'll be in the hospital for at least another forty-eight hours," the doctor said to the police officer.

She was grateful for the doctor's intervention. It gave her a moment to quell the panic that was threatening to overtake her. She stared at the man in the white coat and thought about what he'd just said. Just an hour before, Dr. Jones had told her she could leave tonight. He looked so serious that Liz kept her mouth closed.

The officer nodded and flipped the notebook he was holding shut. Liz bet he was happy to be able to put off the problem for another couple of days. "All right, then. We'll be back tomorrow to discuss how we can protect you, Miss Courtney. You're in a secure wing of the hospital for now. Don't worry about a thing. You should concentrate on feeling better."

It took everything Liz had not to throw something as the officer walked out the door. *Don't worry?* She'd been through hell for the last year. It had started simply. It had been a blind date with a friend of a friend. Tommy Lane had set off a few red flags, and Liz had politely declined his offer for a second date. That should have been the end of it. But one year's worth of creepy phone calls, letters to her boss, and vandalism had finally led to him torching her small townhouse. She had lost everything. It was good to know the police didn't want her to worry.

Liz looked over at the doctor. He was a nice-looking man in his mid-thirties. He'd been kind to her. Everyone in the hospital had gone out of their way to make her feel safe. "Why did you lie to the cop? Is there something else wrong with me?"

Dr. Wright took a deep breath. "You're fine. I lied because I don't want anyone to know where you're going." The door to her room opened, and one of the night nurses walked in. Liz remembered her name was Sandy. She must have changed shifts because it was still light outside. She carried a duffel bag.

"Everything's ready," Sandy said to the doctor.

"Good." The doctor rubbed his hands together and nodded. He turned to Liz, and there was a wealth of sympathy in his eyes. "I'll leave you in Sandy's capable hands. I wish you the best of luck, Ms. Courtney. My card is in that bag. If you need anything, please call me."

Liz watched the doctor exit the room before turning her attention to the nurse. Sandy was an older woman. She looked to be in her mid-fifties and radiated an air of confidence that came with extreme professionalism. She was brisk and efficient, but now she smiled kindly. "Liz, you don't have any family, do you?"

Liz shook her head. Her father had died of cancer ten years ago and her mother in a car accident three years later. She only had an elderly aunt in San Diego. She adored her Aunt Sadie, but she couldn't exactly count on her for protection. Liz had been on her own for a long time, but never before had she felt so isolated and alone. Tommy had done that to her. In the last year, he'd managed to drive off every friend she had.

"I lost my daughter," Sandy said, tears welling as though the loss happened yesterday. "It was ten years ago."

"I'm sorry." Liz murmured all the words she knew she should say. She couldn't imagine how awful it was to lose a child. Losing her parents had been hard enough. Still, her mind was focused on one problem and one problem alone. How was she going to survive when he was still out there?

"Her ex-boyfriend walked into the place she worked and shot her three times in the heart," Sandy explained matter-of-factly. "She'd done all the right things. She got restraining orders, called the cops on him. It didn't matter."

She'd done all the things Liz had done, and she'd still died at the hands of her stalker. Liz felt her whole body tremble. She had nowhere to go. Tommy was very savvy when it came to tracking a person. He could track her with her credit cards or trace her through her cell phone. Once he had found out she'd gone to a bar with some girlfriends and accused her of cheating. He'd left numerous voice mails detailing a relationship that didn't exist. It had proven to Liz that he was completely insane. Liz had been shocked to learn he'd been tracking the license plate on her car as she drove through intersections with cameras. Anywhere she went, he would find her.

Sandy shook her head as though trying to pull herself back into the present. "If she was alive today, I'd tell her to do the one thing I'm telling you to do."

"What?" Liz's tears were falling freely now.

"Run, sweetie." Sandy reached out and took her hands. "You gotta run. Until they have enough evidence to put him in jail, you aren't safe. He'll just come after you again. The nurses took up a collection. There's five thousand dollars in that bag. It's not much, but it's a start. I have a friend who helps out in situations like this. He made you three new driver's licenses and passports. They'll pass the tests. There are social security cards, too. It's everything you need to start a new life."

Liz looked down at the duffel bag and then back up to Sandy. If she had a new identity, maybe he wouldn't be able to find her. He wouldn't know what car to watch for or what name to track on her credit cards. She could start over and leave this nightmare behind. Something like hope was starting to bloom inside her. "Why are you doing this for me?"

Sandy's face was lined with heartache. "I do this for a lot of girls, more than I care to think of. I do this because I wish someone had done it for my daughter."

Two hours later, Liz sat in the front seat of a beat-up sedan. There was a black wig covering her golden brown hair. She had instructions to dye her hair at the earliest opportunity. There was a box of L'Oréal in her bag. Liz smiled slightly as she thought about it. She'd always wanted to try blonde.

"I have a blog at this address." Sandy pressed a piece of paper in Liz's hand. "Check it every week if you can. I'll post information there when I get some. I'll let you know if it's safe to come home, okay?"

Liz nodded, her heart filled with gratitude. These people had given her everything. The doctor had bought this car and then made sure the plates couldn't be traced back to any of them. The day shift nurses had purchased clothes for her. What they had really bought her was a chance at survival. "How can I ever thank you?"

Sandy's smile was watery. "You thank me by living a good life, sweetheart. You go out there, and you find your heart's desire. Don't you let him win. Fall in love and have a bunch of kids and just live. You hear me?"

Liz nodded, unable to stop her own tears. She started the car and waved at the woman who'd given her this completely new life. It was scary. She looked at the entrance to the garage. There was a brilliant light at the end of the tunnel. It led to Amanda Cooper. She was Mandy Cooper now. She had to figure out who that was. Despite the horror of the past year, there was a little excitement in her stomach, like little butterflies that were excited at the prospects opening up to her.

Mandy Cooper drove toward that light, already shedding the vestiges of her old life. She would take the good stuff, her parents' love and the lessons she'd learned, with her. She would toss away everything else. She didn't need it. When she drove into the harsh sun of the Dallas afternoon, she turned her face to the light. The warmth of the sun felt like a benediction on her skin.

She pointed the car toward the highway and didn't look back.

\* \* \* \*

Sheriff Ryan Harper sat on the porch watching Nina pack her cute little convertible. His dog, Quigley, lay at his feet, a tennis ball in his mouth, patiently waiting for someone to toss the nasty old thing. Rye wasn't in the mood to play. If he was half the gentleman his mama had raised him to be, he would get off his butt and help Nina. He tipped back his bottle of beer and watched her. He should have known it wouldn't work.

"You're a bastard, you know." Nina's pretty face was flushed with exertion. She shoved her platinum blonde hair out of her eyes.

Rye shrugged. His Stetson sat low on his forehead. The heat of the Colorado summer was starting to make him sweat. He knew he should get out of his sheriff's uniform when he was drinking, but he couldn't work up the will to care. "I'm not the one running out on my wedding."

Nina sighed. Her shoulders slumped, and she seemed to get smaller. "I'm sorry, Rye. I got a better offer. You know how that goes."

Rye huffed. "Yeah, someone with more money comes along, and you run off chasing him. Don't think you can come back here when it goes bad for you in Denver."

Nina flashed him a superior smile and was right back to being her arrogant self. "I'm never coming back here. I'm going to be a rich man's wife." She leaned against her trunk, seemingly more comfortable now. "Look, Rye, don't take it bad. You know I care about you. I just care about me more."

In the distance, a truck pulled up the long drive. Quigley's tail began to thump. "Didn't you want to be gone before Max got home?"

Nina's brow wrinkled as she took in the sight of that Ford coming up the dirt road. "Damn it, I told you not to call him." She worked overtime shoving suitcases into the car.

"I didn't," Rye said calmly. He knew something Nina didn't know. Max wouldn't care. Rye appreciated Nina's fear too much to tell her differently. "Big Brother just has impeccable timing. He always has."

Nina was trying to get the trunk closed when Maxwell Harper slid out of his old truck. Quigley, drooling around the tennis ball, ran to his master. That old dog knew what Nina didn't. Max had always liked animals more than humans. Max didn't miss a beat. He pulled the ball out of his dog's mouth and threw it as far as he could. Quigley ran off, happy to have found a playmate. Max's eyes slid from his younger brother to the blonde and back again. "The wedding's off, then?"

"Yup."

"Thank God." Max didn't even attempt to hide his relief. He smiled broadly. He wore blue jeans and a neatly pressed shirt. It was what he wore when meeting with clients. Rye took note of the paperwork sticking out of his small laptop bag. At least someone had scored.

"Asshole," Nina spat, looking at the older of the two brothers. "I can't believe I wasted my time on you two. You know what, Ryan Harper? I'm going to give you a piece of advice. If you ever want to get married, you better dump Max. It's fine for a night, or even a couple of months of sex, but no woman is going to put up with his shit. You're going to be alone for the rest of your life if you insist on this perverted lifestyle."

"You didn't think it was perverted last night," Rye replied. Last night she'd seemed pretty damn happy between them. Max had never thought Nina was the one for them, but he hadn't minded fucking her.

"Oh, I thought it was perverted," Nina corrected him. "I just liked it. As a fantasy goes, the whole twin thing is pretty hot. I just can't do it for the rest of my life. What you two want, no woman is going to give you. That's my advice. Oh, and get the hell out of this weird little town. I sure as hell am. Bye." She twirled around, her little shorts hugging her luscious ass.

In a moment, the dust was flying as she drove out of their lives. Rye found himself strangely unmoved by her defection.

"You okay?" Max sank down into the chair beside Rye. He set his bag on the porch and started rocking. It didn't escape Rye's notice that there was a third rocker that sat empty. He'd bought it a couple of years back, hoping that they would find a woman to sit with them.

Nina hadn't been one to sit and enjoy the sunset while rocking on the porch.

Rye shrugged. He wasn't okay, but that had less to do with Nina than he liked to admit. "I didn't love her. I just wanted to start my life. I wanted to get married, have some kids, and just start, I guess." It had started to feel like he was in limbo. He had just turned thirty, and the only marriage prospect he'd had in years was driving off to Denver.

Max got very quiet. "She's probably right, you know. You would do a lot better without me."

"It's not your fault she left, Max." Rye believed it. Max might be surly at times, but he was a genuinely nice guy.

"I think it's time we tried something different," Max said thoughtfully. "You should try dating on your own. I want out for a while. I just want to be alone. I'm not cut out for the long-term thing, Rye."

Rye turned to his twin. "How can you say that?"

Max smiled sadly. Quigley returned with the ball. His massive paws rested on Max's feet. He plopped the dripping ball on Max's lap, and Max quickly began the process all over again.

"I can say that because I'm thirty years old, and I've never been in love. I guess I'm never going to be. It's all right. I've got my work. That's enough."

Rye sighed and cursed the day he met Nina. Now Max was going to brood. The last time a long-term girl walked out, Max had brooded for two years. Max had retreated, and Rye had been left to date on his own. He knew Max didn't love Nina, but rejection was rejection, and Max took it hard.

"We'll see what happens." Rye was the younger twin, but he took the lead when it came to things like this. He wasn't willing to give up. He popped open another beer and scratched his chest. "What do you think she meant when she called this a weird town?"

Max yawned. "I have no idea. It's a great town. It's nice and quiet, except when the Farley boys try to launch those rockets of theirs."

"Don't forget the Wiccans chanting. That can get loud."

"They only do that a couple of times a year. It's the live-action role-playing that I take exception to," Max said with a frown. "Those kids scare my horses. Other than that, we're perfectly normal."

Rye decided not to bring up the nudist colony on the outskirts of town or mention the performance art done in the square every Friday at noon. He smiled to himself. Bliss, Colorado was a weird little town, and he liked it that way. One day some gorgeous woman was going to come through Bliss and like it, too.

He couldn't wait for that day.

# Chapter One

*One Year Later*

It was the weirdest little town.

"Rachel, you have an order up," Hal barked from the kitchen.

"Coming." She was finally getting used to answering to Rachel. She liked her new name. Rachel Swift seemed to suit her in a way that Mandy Cooper hadn't. She was even starting to like it more than Elizabeth Courtney.

Rachel turned from the large windows of the diner where she had been watching Nell and Henry Flanders make their statement about monarchial rule in England. They were making the point through mime, of course. It was Friday, and apparently every Friday Nell and Henry made a political statement. Rachel had only been in Bliss, Colorado for two weeks, but she already looked forward to the Friday lunch show.

Rachel grabbed the burger and fries and looked down at the table number. It was Stella's order, but Stella had walked outside for a quick smoke break. As Stella was the owner of the diner, Rachel didn't complain. She smiled and turned to take the order to table fourteen.

She bit her bottom lip when she saw who was sitting at the small table, looking intently at his papers. Maxwell Harper. Her crazy stupid heart started thudding in her chest. Max Harper was just about the best-looking thing she'd ever seen. He'd walked into the diner the morning after she'd gotten the job, and his stark blue eyes were all she thought about since. Well, she also thought about his broad shoulders and how amazing his butt looked in a pair of jeans.

*Men are bad.* She began the silent litany she went through every time she thought she would break down and throw herself into the cowboy's arms. She was never going to learn. She was on the run from one man. She did not need to beg another to take her. Even if she really, really wanted to.

Besides, she thought as she started toward the table, she wouldn't be here for very long. She hadn't meant to stop in Bliss. She'd run out of money in Alamosa and had just enough gas to get to Bliss. The waitressing gig was a good way to build up some cash, but she couldn't stay in the same place for too long. She hadn't forgotten how close she'd come to getting caught and how fast she'd had to bury Mandy Cooper. She was on the second of three IDs. Rachel didn't like to think what would happen when she ran out of those.

She carefully put the plate down and tried not to sigh when Max's baby blues looked up at her. Men shouldn't have eyelashes like that. He was a work of art. "Is there anything else I can get you?"

He smiled shyly. That got to her, too. He was so polite around her. "I'd like some more Coke, please."

"Of course," Rachel said, her voice way more breathy than she'd intended. She picked up his empty glass. "I'll be right back with it."

Rachel turned and walked toward the drink station. Stella walked in from the back, smoothing the apron over her jeans and white T-shirt.

"How you doing, doll?" The forty-something force of nature winked at Rachel.

"It's going well. The lunch rush seems to have started." Rachel liked Stella Benoit. Stella was in the long slide to fifty, but she was fighting it with everything she had. She was a broad in the best sense of the word. She was loud and assertive, funny and kind. "Table fourteen came up, but I took it out for you."

Stella shoved her lighter in the pocket of her too tight jeans. "Thanks. I swear I'm going to quit one of these days...Wait, oh no, hon, was that Max Harper's order?"

Rachel nodded. She hoped her face hadn't gone gooey at the sound of his name.

Stella's face had gone a little white. "Damn it. I forgot to tell Hal that was for Max. He likes his burgers cooked to an inch of their life. Why he wants to eat a hockey puck, I have no idea, but he'll shout the place down until we get it right." Stella started marching toward the dining room. Rachel gamely followed, carrying Max's refreshed Coke.

"I don't think he'll get upset. He seems perfectly reasonable to me. He's just a little shy." Rachel wasn't sure why, but Stella seemed to think that Max was a time bomb waiting to explode. Now that she thought about it, everyone gave Max a wide berth.

Stella turned on a dime, and Rachel had to stop quickly to avoid running into her. "You're kidding, right? Honey, that man is the bear of the county. Seriously, I have often hoped that someone will shoot him and bring him trussed up to the Big Game dinner we have at the end of the summer. He would probably be too tough to eat. That man is only gentle with horses. If you don't have a long tail attached to your ass, he'll tear you apart when you cross him."

Rachel took a deep breath and continued following her boss. The dining room was filling up. She saw Jen's ponytail bob as she bounced through to shove her orders at the cook. The younger waitress looked over with a questioning glance. Her eyes followed the track of Rachel's movements and grew wide. Rachel watched her shrink back and knew there would be no help from that corner.

"Now, Max, this was my fault and not Rachel's." Stella acted as though she was approaching a dangerous animal who might pounce at the first given sign of attack. She held her hands out. "I got busy and took two orders after yours and forgot to note your preferences."

Max looked from his burger to Stella and then to Rachel. He seemed to make a decision. "It's perfectly fine, Stella. Rachel brought me just what I wanted."

Stella's brows came together to form a perfect V on her forehead. "Max, that damn thing is practically still mooing."

Max waved off her worry. He picked up the burger. "I'm sure it's perfect." He took a big bite. Rachel couldn't help but notice him wince as he bit into the medium-rare burger. He smiled through it. "It's great," he said, choking it down. "And it's got pickles." He coughed. "Love those pickles."

"Have you gone insane?" Stella asked, hands on her hips.

Max discreetly used his napkin to rid himself of the offending pickle. When he looked back at Stella, his face was serene once more. "Nope, I'm perfectly sane. Can't a man change his mind?"

"I'll take it back to the kitchen, and Hal will burn it just the way you like it." Stella reached out to grab the plate.

Max pulled it back defensively. "No. Rachel brought it, and I'm going to eat it."

Stella went still for a moment, then threw back her football-helmet hair. She laughed long and loud. "Damn me, I never thought I'd see the day. I look forward to this, Harper. Paybacks can be hell, you know. Enjoy your undercooked burger, my friend. I'll be sure to note your newfound appreciation for pickles."

Stella turned on her stark white-and-red embroidered cowboy boots and walked off. Rachel felt the weight of just about everyone in the diner staring at her. She set the Coke down on the table.

"I can take it back if you like," Rachel offered with a small grin. He looked a little pale as he tried to eat the burger. Rachel had learned Hal would just lightly sear it if you didn't give him explicit instructions.

He shook his head, and Rachel admired his short, curly brown hair. It was thick with red and gold threaded through the brown. She really wanted to see if it was as soft as it looked. His masculine jaw was starting to show signs of a five o'clock shadow though it was just past noon.

"It's fine. I'm not hard to please." He looked at her directly, and she got the feeling he wasn't talking about the burger. "As a matter of fact, I'm quite easy." He reached out and brushed his hand against hers.

Rachel laughed nervously, her skin tingling where he touched it. She suddenly wondered what it would feel like to have that hand on a more intimate part of her body. It was an awfully big hand. "That's a pretty horse." Rachel changed the subject quickly because the need to sit in his lap had just become almost too much to bear.

He looked down at the file he'd been studying. There was a gorgeous horse in the picture. "Her name is Sunflower. She's a quarter horse, and she's got everything it takes to be an excellent rodeo horse. My client's daughter is a barrel racer."

"But?" There had to be a but. She'd learned a little about Max over the past two weeks. He was very good at training difficult horses.

"Well, she kicks everyone who comes near her." Max's voice was a deep rumble that rolled over her skin. "It makes it hard to train her, so her owner is sending her to me. It's what I do, Rachel. See, deep down, Sunflower is really just scared. She doesn't want to kick and buck every time someone comes near her. She wants love and affection. She wants to please her master. She's just not sure how. That's where I come in. I teach her it's all right to accept love. I gently ease her into the saddle. I show her just how nice it is to let someone special ride her."

Holy crap, she was getting wet in the middle of the diner. It was like his low, sexy voice had a direct line to her pussy, and everything heated up when he started talking.

"Do you like to ride, Rachel?"

Oh, boy, did she like to ride? Not horses, of course, but she definitely wouldn't mind a cowboy. She missed riding. It had been a really long time, and part of her thought she might never ride again. "Sure," was all she managed because her brain was thinking about what it would feel like to ride Max Harper.

Max smiled up at her, a wide grin that made his eyes sparkle. He looked more approachable when he smiled like that. "That's great, Rachel. What kind of horse did you train on?"

"Oh, I've never ridden a horse," she blurted out without thinking.

Max's smile turned distinctly seductive. "Then what type of riding were we talking about, darlin'?"

Rachel swallowed and sought an easy way out. She couldn't do this with him. As gorgeous as he was, she couldn't flirt and pretend that she was this carefree girl. She must never, never forget what was at stake.

"I have to get back to work." She turned away from the hottest man she'd ever met. She walked back to the counter, where Stella was talking to Mel Hughes, the resident conspiracy nut. He lived in a small cabin up the mountain but made the trek almost daily to sit at the diner's counter and visit with Stella. He was completely insane but harmless, Rachel had discovered. He also made the prettiest pottery. Rachel had admired it when she walked through the town's galleries.

"But, Stella, when I left the house I checked the time," Mel insisted. "It was 10:21. When I got to the car, it was 10:35. It does not take me fourteen minutes to get to the car. They took me, I tell you."

Stella looked sympathetic. "Oh, hon, that wasn't an alien abduction. You just can't set your clocks right. I'll come up to your place and make sure all your clocks are in sync, all right?"

Mel leaned in, his voice low and trembling. "Then how do you explain the fact that my backside is very sore in an intimate place? I think they probed me, Stella."

Rachel fought hard not to giggle. She knew exactly what Stella was about to say. They had this little discussion every couple of days. She walked to the counter and opened the bakery plate.

"They didn't probe you," Stella assured him, patting his arm. "You just eat bacon on everything. You need some fiber. Rachel?"

Rachel reached to pass her a bran muffin on a clean plate. She glanced out over the dining room. The muffin fell off the plate as she was completely shocked to see Max Harper talking to a perfect replica of himself.

"Oh my God," she said in utter horror. "There's two of him."

Without missing a beat, Stella got a new muffin. She looked cheery as she followed Rachel's sight line. "Don't worry about it, hon. You won't have to pick. The rumor is they like to share."

"Not helpful," Rachel said in a daze. It wasn't helpful at all.

\* \* \* \*

"Hey, bro," a familiar voice said. Max looked up and saw Rye walking in. He nodded and winked at a couple of the regulars before turning a chair around to straddle it with his long legs. He was wearing his sheriff's uniform and requisite Stetson. Max's twin politely took his hat off and set it to the side.

"How was Colorado Springs?" Max asked. He wished Rye was still there. He hadn't expected his brother back for another two days. He'd been attending training sessions at some bigwig crime-fighter convention.

"Boring." Rye leaned forward and stole a fry. "I could barely stay awake during the lectures on the new traffic laws. Seriously, couldn't they just give me a pamphlet or something? Three hours of some DPS dude droning on just about killed me. You gonna eat that?" Rye reached out and grabbed the burger. It was halfway down his throat before Max could give his assent.

"Feel free," Max told his baby brother. "Baby brother" was a misnomer. Rye was exactly two and a half minutes younger than Max, but he was never allowed to forget it. Max pushed the plate toward Rye. He didn't care about the burger. He was still thinking about Rachel.

He'd come on too strong. He should have known better. He should have taken it easier. She was nervous around him, and he'd come on to her like a horny bull. He'd been very careful around Rachel Swift up to this point. For two whole weeks, he'd watched his temper around her. He'd been excruciatingly polite to everyone in her vicinity. It hadn't been all that hard. His anger issues seemed to take a nosedive when Rachel's sweet face was around.

Rye continued talking about something to do with his job. Max just nodded and kept his eyes discreetly on Rachel.

He watched her awkwardly step around the counter, obviously still disturbed by their conversation. He hadn't been able to help himself. He needed to make sure she was aware of him. Well, she was definitely aware. Max let his fingers drum against the table. It wasn't that she was uninterested. Max was experienced enough to know when a woman was intrigued. Rachel was curious about him. She was just nervous. He was a big guy with a bad rep and an even worse temper. He had to show her he could control himself around her.

He thought back to that first day and couldn't help the smile that came with the memory. She'd been nervous that day, too. She'd dropped a plate and looked surprised Stella hadn't fired her on the spot. Max could have told her Stella was very patient with the strays she took in. Max might fight with Stella from time to time, but he respected the lady. She was good people.

Rachel had looked grateful to have a job. She'd cleaned up the mess and come to his table. She'd carefully taken his order, writing everything he said down on her little pad. She'd chewed on that bottom lip of hers. God, he loved her lips. They were perfect and pouty, and his dick would look so good between them.

Max took a long drink of cold Coke and told himself to settle down. He had been walking around in a permanent state of erection ever since Rachel Swift had walked up to his table and asked him sweetly if there was anything she could do for him.

She could lie down beneath him and spread her legs, that's what she could do. She could spread those pretty, petite legs of hers and show him her pussy. He'd stare at it for a while because there was just nothing more beautiful than a ripe and ready pussy. He'd lie on his stomach and arrange her legs over his shoulders and make a meal of her. Rye would watch...

*Damn it.* He had to get that out of his head. His hands fisted in frustration. They weren't doing that anymore. They were going to be perfectly normal from now on. They weren't going to scare off good prospects with their perverse needs. It had been a year since the last time they had played out their ménage fantasies. Rye had tried dating without him. He'd seen some girl from Creede for a while, but broke it off. Max hadn't dated at all. He'd buried himself in work. Rachel was the first girl to catch Max's interest.

*Don't you fool yourself. You aren't interested in Rachel. You're half in love with her.* For the first time in his thirty-one years, he was falling in love.

"Are you even listening to me, Max?" Rye's voice cut through Max's thoughts. "And what the hell is going on around here? This burger is actually edible. It's nice and juicy. What's wrong with this picture?"

This was why he wished Rye was still far, far away. Max tried hard not to flush. He needed to play this very cool. "They just got the order wrong. It's no big deal."

Rye's mouth hung open for a minute. "Do we need to call in a doctor? Wait a minute. Is Stella still alive, or did you stuff her body in the trash compactor? I have ways of finding out these things, you know."

Max pointed to the counter. "Stella's alive and well and trying to talk Mel out of his latest paranoid fantasy."

It was a mistake. Max realized it the moment he said it. Rachel stood right beside her boss. Those big green eyes were even bigger than usual as she stared at the two of them. For a moment, she looked like a kid who'd found the last cupcake on the planet. Then she obviously realized they were looking back because she suddenly looked intently interested in wiping down the counter.

Max turned to his brother, and sure enough, Rye's face had gone slack. "No," Max said. He set his jaw stubbornly. "I saw her first."

Rye didn't bother to look back at his brother. He just stared at the beauty with strawberry blonde hair. "But I saw her best, Max. You got a date with her, yet?"

"No, I'm working my way up to it," Max explained, trying to salvage the situation. "There's something up with her. She's very nervous."

Rye's smile was brimming with self-assurance as he stood up and straightened his jacket. "You make a lot of women nervous, Max. Watch how it's done, Big Brother."

"Damn it, Rye." But his twin was already making his way to the counter. Max stood up and followed. He was going to beat the crap out of the town sheriff if he scared Rachel off.

"Hello there, sweetheart." Rye poured on the charm.

Stella snorted and muttered something under her breath before walking off to check the kitchen.

Max watched as Rachel really looked at his brother for the first time. He noticed her mouth tighten as she took in his uniform. It was another clue. He'd wondered if she was running from something. She had that look. He needed to make her comfortable, and then she would tell him what was wrong. He'd fix it, and they could have raucous sex to celebrate her freedom from whatever was bugging her. That was his plan. Now his brother was fucking up his perfectly fine plan.

"What can I get for you, Officer?" Rachel pulled out her ever-present notepad and a little pen. She was very professional.

Rye was not. "Oh, I think I can come up with a few things you could get me. How about your phone number? That way I can call you, and we can plan out our date."

Max was satisfied when Rachel looked completely unmoved by his brother's charm. "I don't have a phone."

Rye's eyebrows shot up. "What do you mean you don't have a phone? Everybody's got a phone, darlin'. Most people have at least two."

"I don't have one," she said dully. Max didn't like the look in her eyes. It was like all the life in them had fled at the sight of Rye's badge. "Is that a crime, Officer?"

"It's Sheriff." Now Rye's voice held a little uncertainty. Max knew it had been a long time since a girl turned down Sheriff Ryan Harper. Max watched as the doubt in Rye's face dissolved, and he gave her his high-wattage grin. "My name is Ryan Harper, but everyone calls me Rye. I see you've met my brother."

She nodded at Max, but it was a polite thing. It held none of the shy curiosity from before. He was going to bash his brother's skull in.

"Is there anything you wanted from the kitchen, Sheriff Harper?" Rachel asked. "I have other customers waiting."

Rye scratched his head, and Max saw the moment he decided to retreat. "No, darlin'. I just wanted to say hello. It was nice to meet you." His eyes flashed to her name tag. "Rachel. If you have any trouble, you give me a call, okay?"

Max followed Rye back to the table, where he sat down. His brother looked thoughtful as he munched on the burger he'd stolen. Max ate the fries as he waited for Rye's brain to work through the problem.

"That girl's in trouble, bro," Rye finally said.

"No shit, Sherlock." Max was damn glad there weren't many crimes to solve in Bliss.

"Damn." Rye sighed. "I hate it when I have to arrest someone that fine."

Max tried to pin his brother with his most intimidating stare. "You are not arresting her, you understand me? If she's done something, then I'll take care of it. How bad could it possibly be? She can't weigh more than 110 pounds. I don't see her committing a bunch of violent crimes at her size."

"Yeah." Rye stared at Rachel as she took orders from a table of tourists. "She's really pretty, but she could use a couple of decent meals."

"You should have seen her two weeks ago."

She'd been sickly thin. At first, Max wondered if she was one of those girls who eschewed food in order to look as skinny as possible. Her first break had set that out of his mind. Waitresses at Stella's ate for free one meal per shift. Rachel had inhaled a chicken salad sandwich and a bowl of vegetable soup. She'd practically cried when Stella set a piece of chocolate pie in front of her. He'd wanted to scoop her up, take her back to the house, and make sure she never missed another meal again.

"She's running then?" Rye asked.

"I think so." Max could use his brother's help on that part. Rye had resources that Max didn't. If Rachel was on the run from something, it would be good to know what might come after her.

Rye nodded. "I'll see what I can turn up. You really like this girl?"

"I do," Max said quietly. It was odd to think about seeing a woman without Rye. Rachel was special, though. He had to see where it was going.

Rye was quiet for a long time. His blue eyes were sad as he turned back to his brother. "I'll back off, then. I just want you to be happy, man."

Rye was quiet as he finished off the burger. Max put down the fries. He took another drink and contemplated his situation. His twin was sometimes more like the other half of himself than a brother. He wondered if he could ever be happy as half a man.

# Chapter Two

Rachel breathed a sigh of relief as Jen finished ringing up Max Harper. He tipped his hat toward her, and then he and his brother walked out the door. Jen immediately turned and joined her at the counter. Stella was hot on Jen's heels.

"That man is crazy about you." Stella slapped her well-manicured hand on the counter.

"I don't know what you're talking about. He's just a customer." Rachel felt the slightest bit cornered.

"Just a customer?" Jen asked. "He's practically become a tenant. He's eaten breakfast, lunch, and dinner here every day for two weeks."

"He didn't do that before?"

"Not at all. He changed his habits the day I hired you." Stella had a knowing smile on her face. "You could do worse, you know. Max and I have a love-hate relationship, you see."

"She loves to hate him," Jen supplied with a grin. She was all of twenty-two, with bright eyes and a positive outlook on everything. She was an artist, a painter trying to get her work in some of the local galleries.

"Now," Stella began, patting her helmet of bright blonde hair, "you know that's just because our sexual chemistry is hard to resist. If I were ten years younger, I would tame that man. He would be a little puppy coming to my hand after I got through with him."

Jen snorted. "Max Harper was never a puppy."

Rachel watched the two women. They seemed to have the scoop on everyone and everything that went on in Bliss. "He seems really sweet to me."

"He is sweet," Jen replied. "He just has a real crusty exterior. He's one of those men who yells a lot, but that's because he's trying to cover up for the fact that he's just a big softy underneath it."

Stella nodded sagely. "It's true. When I called him the bear of the county, I probably should have added 'teddy' to the 'bear' part. Max complains when things aren't perfect. He's a picky man. But when the chips are down, you can count on him. Even when he was feuding with Hank Farley over his storage units encroaching on Max's land, Max was the first one to help out when he had a stroke and couldn't afford his hospital bills. Rye might be the charmer, but Max is the sweet one."

Jen poured herself a cup of coffee and took a long drink. Rachel saw her pretend not to notice when Stefan Talbot walked in. Rachel could tell Jen had a crush on the handsome painter. She always asked to switch with Rachel when he sat in her section.

"Rye isn't exactly sour. He spent a weekend worth of his free time fixing my car because I couldn't afford the shop." Jen sighed. "I'll tell you, Rach, if I thought I could handle it, I would give those brothers a try myself."

"So, they just openly share women?" Rachel asked, a little surprised. It was kind of taboo in her mind. It was totally sexy and hot, but she would think people would look down on it.

Stella waved off the statement. "We don't judge people here in Bliss, hon. Too many of us came here to get away from prying eyes, if you know what I mean. We tend to accept people the way they are. We're kind of a community of free spirits. Tolerance is our catchphrase. How else would we get along with all those nudists?"

"You know you love them," Jen teased.

"I do. I just wish they would shave more often than they do. I swear some of those men are responsible for the numerous sightings of Bigfoot we get around here."

Rachel laughed and got back to work. The whole rest of her shift she was assaulted with numerous facts about the Harper twins. Now she knew way more about the hot brothers than she probably wanted to. They were infamous in southern Colorado for being wild in their youth. All of that had changed when their mother died of a sudden heart attack and their father walked away, unable to deal with it. They ended up raising their younger sister. Rye had taken a job, and Max set about saving his family's stables. Twelve years later, Brooke Harper was about to graduate from college, and the men were thriving professionally. It wasn't as great on the personal front.

*At least something is working for them*, Rachel thought as she prepared to leave the diner. She grabbed her purse and waved goodbye to Stella and Jen. She walked out to her car and felt weary at the thought of the long hours ahead. She was tired of running. She was tired of being afraid every minute of the day. She wanted something for herself, even if it was temporary.

Twenty minutes later, Rachel pulled her car into a small clearing surrounded by a cluster of trees. She put the battered Jeep in park and got out. She was happy to see the little pond was completely empty. She made one careful sweep of the area and then got the soap and shampoo out of the back. Living out of her car had its disadvantages. It had been weeks since she'd been able to afford a motel room for the night, so she had to make do. One of the lovely things about Bliss was the numerous little ponds and lakes that dotted the county. This particular pond was her favorite. It was tiny, isolated, and crystal clear. The sun warmed the water, but in the middle, it was still chilly.

Rachel quickly got out of her jeans and T-shirt as she thought about the events of the day. Meeting Ryan Harper had thrown her for a loop. Max was one thing. He trained horses. A sheriff was a completely different animal. Rachel walked into the cool water with absolutely no thought to her nudity. This place was a little piece of paradise. There was something about Bliss that made her lose her inhibitions. It felt right to be naked in the sunlight here. She sighed and went under the water. When her hair was wet and she'd gotten used to the temperature, she surfaced. She let herself float, looking into the clear blue sky. It was never that clear back in Dallas. There was always too much smog. Rachel had never considered herself anything but a city girl. Being in Bliss was changing her mind.

Bliss was a wonderful place. She'd been in a lot of cities and towns over the last year, but none of them made her want to stay the way Bliss did. She loved the mountains. She loved the quirky streets with their art galleries and boutiques and even an old-fashioned trading post. The little town got a lot of tourist attention for being an art mecca. Artists from all over southern Colorado showed their work in Bliss's galleries. There was even a real, true repertory theater. Rachel didn't have the money to go see a show, but she wished she did. She felt like this was a place where she could fit in. She even loved the weird citizens. Mel was a hoot when he wasn't worried about aliens taking over the government. Nell and Henry were friendly even as they fought with Stella. They were trying to get her carnivorous boss to give them vegan choices on the menu. Jen was very sweet and loved to paint. Yes, she liked the locals just fine.

The sudden thought of Max and Rye was almost too much to handle. It had been a long time since she had wanted a real, live man, much less two. There was a time when that had been her biggest fantasy, two gorgeous men pleasuring her. Then Tommy had happened, and her biggest fantasy had become surviving the day with all her body parts still attached. Rachel shook her head. She wasn't going to think about him. This was her time, and if she wanted to fantasize about her sweet cowboy, she would. She would think about Max. Rye was far too dangerous. She wouldn't get near another cop.

But Max was a different story.

A small noise pulled Rachel out of her thoughts and sent her scrambling. She forced her feet to the bottom of the pond and covered herself to her neck in the water. Her eyes darted around, looking for the threat. Adrenaline started pumping through her body. Had Tommy found her?

"I'm sorry." Max Harper sat astride the back of a big black horse. Both the man and the animal were powerful creatures. There was an enormous dog at the horse's side. If she didn't know better, she would almost think the dog was a pony. "I was just taking Maverick and Quigley out for some exercise." He was watching her with wide eyes, and she could see his breath hitch in his chest.

She took a long breath to try to slow her thudding heart. She should still be afraid. She was still alone with a man she'd only known for a brief time. So why was she so sure she was okay with Max? *Play it safe. Ask him to leave. Put on your clothes and move on. You're a terrible judge of men.*

But she wasn't. She'd realized there was something wrong with Tommy the minute she met him. She'd done everything right. She'd refused to see him again. Every instinct she had told her Max was different. Max was special. Tommy Lane had taken just about everything from her. Was she going to let him take this, too?

Desire started to course through her veins like a drug. He was right there, and he looked perfect. She had wanted something for herself, and, like a genie granting wishes, he'd shown up. Rachel smoothed back her hair. It was time to make a decision. She might not be in Bliss for long, but she was going to enjoy herself for once. It had been years since she felt a man's body beside hers. She wanted that with Max.

"Do you want me to leave?"

Pulling together every bit of bravado she had, she walked out of the pond, revealing her body to him. "No, Max. I don't want you to leave. I just want you."

* * * *

Max tried to think of one good reason he shouldn't get down off the horse and take Rachel in his arms.

Unfortunately, he thought of about a dozen, the chief one being it was far too soon to make love to her. In her mind, it would just be sex. He had no doubt about that. She would be using him for comfort, pleasure, whatever she was lacking. He would be making love to the woman he was pretty sure he was falling in love with. There was an imbalance in the scenario. If he got off the horse and buried himself in her, he would be at a distinct disadvantage for the rest of their relationship.

Yet, even as he told himself all the reasons to be patient, he was dismounting. His dick wasn't willing to listen. He was rock hard, and the sight of her gorgeous body emerging from the pond like Venus was making his heart thud in his chest. She was the most beautiful thing he'd ever seen.

*What is it about this woman?* She was lovely, but then he knew that he'd been with women that other men would think were more attractive than Rachel. So why did she call to him?

Quigley nosed his leg, and Max looked down. The old mutt had a stick in his mouth. In his mind, it was playtime. Max wasn't on top of Maverick, so this was supposed to be Quigley time.

"Is he part horse?" Rachel's eyes sparkled as she watched the big dog.

Max patted the dog's head. "You might think so. We think he's part Great Dane and part Saint Bernard. He's all pussy, though. I swear I've never seen a more docile dog. Q, go rest, buddy," Max pointed to where he'd left his horse. The dog whined and drooled around his stick. Max prayed he wasn't drooling as much as Quigley, but he didn't hold out much hope.

There was an amused grin on her plump lips as he approached. "Why do they say you're difficult, Max?"

"Because I'm a bastard," he answered honestly. He was a picky, contrary, argumentative bastard, and he didn't really apologize for it.

She laughed. The sound was magical to his ears. "You apparently love dogs and horses. I haven't seen anything that tells me you're a jerk. You've been nothing but sweet around me."

He shrugged, his eyes devouring the sight of her breasts. They were round and soft. They bounced when she walked. The nipples were hard little raspberries. "I've been very careful around you. I don't want to scare you away. I promise, Rachel, I'll always be careful with you."

She frowned, her pouty mouth turning down. "Max, I want you. I want to have sex with you. But I'm not a long-term girl. You have to understand that."

But she was, and Max knew it. She was the type of girl you fell in love with and married. He put her age at roughly thirty. She should have fallen for some professional and had a few precious babies by now. It was the way things went for women like Rachel. Something had happened to throw her life off the rails. He needed to get it back on track because he intended to be the man she fell for.

"Sweetheart, why don't you get dressed, and I'll take you out to dinner?" Max suggested against his penis's wishes. He needed to woo her before he took her. He wanted to romance her and give her the courtship she deserved. He needed her to trust him. "We can talk and get to know each other."

Her face flushed. She was very pale, with delicate skin. She couldn't hide her emotions, and Max realized he'd made a mistake. She nodded and purposefully walked back into the pond to cover her body up.

The smile on her face didn't come anywhere close to her eyes. "I'm not really hungry, Max. I'll just stay here for a while. See you around."

She pointedly swam away from him, and Max knew he'd been dismissed. If he walked away, she might be friendly, but she'd never offer herself again. He'd tried to get it done his way. It looked like he was going to have to use hers.

Max kicked off his boots, then pulled his shirt over his head. Maverick was standing by the pond, calmly waiting for his master to finish with the female so they could continue the exercise. Maverick was a gelding and Quigley had been fixed years back. *Life must be so much simpler for them.* Max eased off his jeans carefully. His raging erection was eager to be set free. The crown of his cock was already weeping with pre-cum.

Rachel surfaced and was treading water. Her light green eyes were wary as she took him in. "What are you doing, Max?"

He put his hands on his hips. He had no real problem with nudity. He'd grown up in this weird little town, and while he had quirks of his own, he'd always accepted himself. It was the best gift Bliss had given him. "I'm about to take a swim in a really cold pond with a woman who just wants me for my body. I'm desperate, though, and I don't have a whole lot of self-respect."

She frowned, reminding him of a gorgeous water nymph. "This is my pond. Go find your own."

Max felt his lips quirk up in a little half grin. "This is my land, darlin'. I'm afraid I own the pond you're currently occupying."

"Oh," she said, her mouth forming a perfect O. His penis got even harder as he thought about that sultry mouth around his cock. The damn thing was standing up straight, lying almost flat against his belly. If he didn't do something soon, it was going to come off his body and seek her out itself. Max strode into the water and dove under the instant he could.

The water was clear, so it was easy to swim toward his lovely target. Her legs were barely touching the bottom of the pond. He loved the curves of her hips and ass. He surfaced, letting his arms wind around her slender waist, forcing her a little deeper so she had to cling to him. It was easy to do. He had a good foot on her petite frame. Her arms instinctively went around his neck.

"Max!"

He smiled. "What? I can't swim in my own pond?"

She pushed at his broad shoulders. "I don't need your pity, Max. Let me go."

Now it was his turn to frown. He brushed his rigid erection against her pussy. "Darlin', this water is cold, but I'm harder than I've ever been in my life. I don't pity you. I've been like this for two damn weeks. If anyone needs some pity, it's me."

"You didn't want me a minute ago." Even as she made the accusation, she cuddled close to him.

She felt so perfect in his arms. They fit together like pieces of a puzzle. Max knew he was never going to want to let her go. "I want way more than you're willing to give me, Rachel, and you know it. I want to be your man. I'm crazy about you."

"You don't even know me," she replied, burrowing her nose into his neck.

Max kissed her ear gently. She was starving for affection, and he intended to drown her in it. "I don't know anything about you?"

"You have no idea where I was born or who my parents are." She practically purred against him.

"You could tell me." She was silent on the subject, so he moved on. "I might not know all the facts and details, but I've learned a lot about you. I know you like chocolate and don't put anything in your coffee. You're a dog person, but you'll put up with cats. You smile at everyone, and there's a light inside you that always makes them smile back. You love music. You can't stop your right foot from tapping when the jukebox comes on. When you know the words, you sing them, and you don't even know you're doing it. You take your work very seriously even though you know you're too smart to be stuck as a waitress for the rest of your life. You'll do that job with everything you have. You're a good person, Rachel."

She pulled back to look at him. There were tears swimming in her eyes. "How could you see so much?"

He used one hand to wipe the tears away. He was very solemn. He didn't intend to play any games with her. "Because I knew I was crazy about you the moment I saw you."

"Don't," she said, her voice catching on the word. "I can't. I can't do anything serious, Max. Please, I just want to lose myself for a little while. Can you give me that?"

He looked at her solemnly. She was practically begging him not to push her. "For now."

Anticipation thrummed through his body as he pulled her close and, for the first time, pressed his lips to hers. She was soft and willing. Her mouth flowered open under his. Max pulled her tightly to him. He loved the way her breasts pressed against the hardness of his chest. He kept the kiss light, letting her set the pace. He needed her so badly, but he held his own desire firmly in check. She needed this even more than he did, and he knew it. After a moment's sweet play, he groaned as he felt her tentatively lick along the seam of his lips.

Max growled as he lost a bit of his control, and he wound his hands in her hair. It was soft against his callused fingers. He held her gently, but with firm intent as he plundered her mouth. He let his tongue plunge in a naked imitation of what his cock wanted to do. He slanted over and over her mouth, their lips meshing together. She felt so right in his arms.

"Oh God, Max," she moaned when he came up for air. "It's been so long."

"How long?" Max didn't really care. She could have been with twelve guys yesterday. As long as he was the last man standing, he'd be satisfied.

"Years." There was a little bit of wonder in her voice. Max was fascinated with the way she was looking at him. It made him feel like a much better man than he'd ever thought he could be. "Like this? Maybe never."

"Good." He lifted her up, bringing her breasts to his mouth. "God, you're beautiful, baby." He sucked a pink nipple into his mouth.

Rachel groaned, and her back bowed as she offered herself to him. He curled his tongue around the peak of her soft breast and thought he would come then and there when she wrapped her legs around his waist. He felt her hot pussy against his skin. He moved between both breasts, not wanting either one to feel left out. She shivered when he bit down gently on her nipple.

Rachel moved restlessly against him, and he knew she was getting hot and bothered. He needed to get her off, because the minute he sank his cock into her, he feared he would explode. He didn't want to leave her unsatisfied. Max turned her around in his arms, palming her breasts as her head fell back against his shoulder. Her ass rubbed against his torso.

"Please touch me," Rachel moaned.

Max anchored her with one hand around her waist and let his other hand trail down to her wet, ripe pussy. He delved into the soft curls there. He wished he could see it, but promised himself that he would have her laid out on his bed soon. He would spread her wide and take his time learning every inch of her. He would cover her with his mouth and taste that hot cunt while she took Rye in her mouth.

Max shook his head, trying to banish the mental image. They were playing it straight this time. He wanted Rachel, and he would have to take her on her terms. As much as he'd loved sharing women with his other half, he had to move on. Max slid his fingers over her pulsing pussy, rubbing her little clit through the soft nest of curls he found. Rachel pushed her pelvis against his questing fingers.

"Yes, Max," she whispered.

Max picked up the pace. He rubbed tight circles with his thumb over her clit while he worked his middle finger into the blinding heat of her cunt. She was so fucking tight. She was going to feel like heaven wrapped around his cock.

"It feels so good." Rachel turned her head up. Max took the invitation and plunged his tongue into her perfect mouth as he fucked her with his fingers. His dick was denting the soft flesh of her ass, and he longed to be able to tunnel his way into her ass. He held off, sensing she was a virgin there. He would have to be careful and prepare her.

Rachel bucked against his fingers, and he felt a warm rush as she came. His cock was throbbing. He couldn't fight it anymore. He quickly turned her around.

"Wrap your legs around my waist," he ordered.

Her face was flushed and she looked sleepy, but she complied with a sexy little smile. "That was fantastic, Max."

He kissed her as he arranged her legs to his liking. She looked like a completely content kitten. "I'm glad I could help, baby."

She traced the line of his jaw with her fingertips. "You're different. A woman could feel safe with you, Max."

She sounded so hesitant, his heart clenched. He wondered who had put that fear in her voice. He made his own voice very gentle. "You are safe with me, Rach. I'll take care of you."

She reached down between them, and her small hand stroked his desperate cock. He couldn't help the tortured hiss that came out when she squeezed the crown.

"Take care of me now, Max," she demanded, her green eyes practically challenging him.

Max's hands tightened on the cheeks of her ass. His dick knew just where to go, and he unerringly found her slick entrance. Rachel steadied herself, placing her hands on his shoulders. Her eyes went wide as Max began working his big cock into her. He started with shallow little strokes. She was so tight that he had to be careful with her. He eased her up and down on his dick, the buoyancy of the water aiding his work. Rachel pushed against him.

*She isn't one to lay back.* Max's latest stroke pushed him in all the way to his balls. He groaned at the exquisite sensation. Rachel was fighting for her pleasure, and Max thought it was the sexiest thing he'd ever seen.

Her little nails were going to leave a mark, he realized with a savage satisfaction. Her mouth was open, and he felt her pussy clench again and again around his cock as she went over the edge.

Max held nothing back after she came. He pounded into her, slamming her slick pussy up and down on his dick. He shoved his way into her until he could feel the cheeks of her ass hitting his balls. He tightened his hold on her as he felt his orgasm start as a tingle at the base of his spine. He slammed her down and held her close as he ground against her, shooting hot cum deep into her welcoming body. His mind felt languid and drugged with pleasure. He kissed her over and over as he softened inside her.

Max was shaking as he realized what he had done. "Oh, shit, Rachel. I am so sorry. I didn't use a condom, baby. I can't believe I did that."

But she just let her head drift down onto his shoulder. "It's okay. I finished my period two days ago. Next time, we need to use one."

He relaxed a little. He was happy there would be a next time. His cock was still pressed against her pussy. "I'm safe, baby. I had a checkup last year, and I haven't been with anyone since."

"Seriously?" She sounded surprised.

"Yes, Rachel," he replied, hugging her to him. "You're the first woman I've wanted in a long time."

Her eyes were heavy as she grinned at him. "I'm glad." She shrieked a little and pointed at a spot behind his head. "What is that?"

Max turned quickly, every instinct screaming at him to protect his woman. He looked at the massive dog who should be barking a warning. Quigley just yawned and relaxed at Maverick's feet. There would be no help from there. Rachel clung to his back, covering her nudity.

"Don't mind us," the intensely hairy man said as he walked by the pond with a friend. "We're just on a nature walk."

Sure enough, the two men had walking sticks in their hands and binoculars around their necks. Other than that, they wore hiking boots and nothing else. Max shook his head. Rye was going to have to remind those nudists where the boundaries of their property ran.

He turned back to Rachel, hoping their Peeping Toms hadn't ruined her mood. He was surprised to find her laughing.

"Stella was right. Bigfoot does roam these woods." She reached out underwater and stroked his cock. It was already getting hard again. "But, Max, Bigfoot's got nothing on you."

He pulled her close and proceeded to prove her point.

# Chapter Three

Rye Harper sat behind his desk and considered the numerous problems Rachel Swift had brought into his peaceful life. So peaceful it was boring, he sighed inwardly. Rachel was the most exciting thing to happen to him in a long time. The only problem was Rachel hadn't happened to him. She'd happened to Max.

The phone rang out at his secretary's desk. "Callie! Phone!" Rye yelled from the comfort of his little office.

A short figure with dark hair flew past the open door in her attempt to get to the phone. She was pushing her smart little glasses further up on her nose. "Got it!" she screamed before she answered the phone. "Bliss County Sheriff's Department." Her voice was now brisk and professional.

Rye listened for a second while drumming his fingers along the desktop.

"No, Mel, I'm so sorry. I really don't have any CIA connections," Callie was saying in a soothing voice. It could only mean one thing.

Rye let his head fall to the desk. He would have to go out to Mel's and pretend to check for bugs again. If he didn't, the old fellow would sit in Stella's diner for hours telling anyone and everyone who came in that Bliss was a focal point for the coming invasion. The locals might ignore him, but he tended to freak out the tourists, and it was tourist season. The last thing he needed was to get called into another meeting of the Bliss County Chamber of Commerce, where he regularly got raked over the coals.

He thought back to last night, when Max had come home late with the dippiest grin on his face. Rye had known in an instant that his brother had fucked Rachel Swift, and probably more than once. Max had the look of a well-satisfied man. He also had the look of a man who'd fallen completely in love. Rye couldn't help it. He was brutally jealous of his brother's happiness.

Maybe it wasn't the same for Max as it was for him. For as long as he could remember, Rye had always fallen for the same girls as Max. It was almost like there was a link between them. When Max saw something he liked, Rye was sure to follow. It explained the deep connection he felt to her the minute he'd met her. Rye had known the instant he looked at the pretty waitress that she was important. He might not be able to read Max's every thought, but when his brother felt something deeply, Rye felt it, too.

Max had been serious about going the vanilla route. Rye had tried to get him interested in Janine, the hot brunette from Creede, but Max wouldn't go for it. Now, it looked like Max was ready to start his life, and Rye was going to be left alone. It wasn't the way he'd envisioned his life. Always in the back of his mind, he'd thought that they would find one woman and settle down. For a while he'd thought that woman would be Nina, but now, looking at Rachel, he knew that had been a mistake. Nina was too hard to ever be at the center of their ménage. She would have taken everything they had and given nothing back.

"Hey, boss." Callie interrupted his thoughts, and he lifted his head off the desk.

Rye tried to look like he wasn't moping. "Yeah, I know. I gotta get my ass out to Mel's and look for alien technology. Get the Detector 3000."

Callie snorted. "I'll make sure to get that for you. I'll also tell Stefan that we'll need to move up to the 4000 model soon. Mel is worried because alien technology apparently changes often."

Stefan Talbot was an artist who worked with everything from oils on canvas to metals. He'd been the one to come up with the idea of the Detector 2000. It was a Wii controller with some modifications. It had some lights and made some high-tech sounds. Mel had been impressed but after six months had wondered if there wasn't an even more sophisticated device. Aliens were tricky little bastards.

"I'll let him know," Rye said. He reached out for his hat. "Anything else? Did Logan go out and talk to the nudists?" Max had pitched a small fit about it last night, and Rye had made a note to send his deputy out to handle it. Rye attributed the fact that the fit was such a small thing to his brother's state of sexual satisfaction. He wondered briefly how he was going to handle it when Rachel started staying the night at their house. How was he going to stand sleeping alone when his brother was right next door, fucking the woman of their dreams?

"Yes, and they prefer to be called naturists." Callie's mother had run the naturist community for years. It was Callie who always reminded him to be tolerant toward the clothing-challenged. "Logan went out this morning, and it's a good thing, too. We've had four reports of 503's since yesterday afternoon."

Rye groaned. A 503 was Bliss County's code for a naked penis sighting. A 504 referred to naked females, but strangely, almost no one ever called that in. "Yeah, they're all about the nature walk right now. It's wildflower time. I just hope they don't go too high into the mountains. I would hate for the damn bears to try to mate with one of them."

Callie laughed. "I was talking to Bill, and he was really excited about all the activities they have planned for the summer. You should know that the men are planning a warrior-in-the-buff outing. There'll be lots of chanting and drumming."

The sheriff sighed. Bill Hartman owned the land the commune was on. Rye was just about to give him a call when he noticed how enthused Callie looked. Callie loved that commune and all the people who lived there. They had made sure her mother had been comfortable while she lost her long-term battle with cancer. Callie was perfectly comfortable spending a lot of her free time with the naturists. Rye shook his head as he looked at the woman who was as close to him as a sister. He always made sure he called before he showed up at her cabin to avoid getting a show. "Put it on the calendar, please. And remind me to buy some industrial-strength earplugs. If they keep Max awake, he'll make the bears look soft and cuddly." If he even noticed over all the noise Rye was sure Rachel made. She looked like a screamer. The quiet ones were always tigers in bed.

"I heard Max has a new girl." Callie's tone was soft, and Rye heard sympathy creeping into her voice. "You okay with that?"

Callie had been his assistant for five years. She'd taken the job when he became the sheriff. Rye knew not much got by Callie Sheppard.

"Sure," Rye lied, plastering a smile on his face. "I think it's great that Max is happy."

He felt her eyes on him. It was the look of a too perceptive little sister figuring out exactly what her big brother didn't want her to discover. Callie shook her head. "Do you really think this whole 'dating apart' thing will work out? Don't you think you're fighting your nature a bit?"

"Tell Max that," Rye said morosely. He didn't even try to keep things like that from Callie. She tended to see through him. "He doesn't think I'll ever find what I want as long as he's around. Then he goes out and finds Rachel."

"And you like her, too." Callie's brown eyes watched him, studying his responses. At times like this, she reminded him of a cute little owl.

Rye shrugged. "She's okay, I guess."

"Right," she said, seemingly unconvinced.

Callie started to play with her shoulder-length brown hair. Rye knew that look. Callie knew something and wasn't sure she should tell. Callie was the worst gossip in the county, and it looked like Rachel was already on her radar.

"Spit it out."

Callie bit her bottom lip, and her eyes slid away from his face. "I don't know if I should."

Rye was unwilling to play games. He wanted to know what was up with Rachel. It was obvious she was in trouble, and he needed to be ready for it. She belonged to Max, and Max's happiness was important to Rye. "Tell me, or you're fired."

Callie rolled her eyes. "I'm terrified of that threat. Fine. It isn't anything bad. Rachel seems like a real sweet girl. I just think she's lying about a few things. She told Stella she was staying at the motel on the outskirts of town."

Rye shrugged and released a breath he hadn't realized he'd been holding. "That's not so bad. It's clean, at least."

"That's just it, Rye," Callie continued. "I talked to Gene just yesterday. He'd never heard of her. That motel is his baby. Even if he hadn't checked her in himself, do you honestly believe he wouldn't remember her name?"

No, he didn't believe that for a second. Why would Rachel lie about where she was staying? He thought about the trace he'd put on her earlier this morning. He'd put her name into the system along with her plate number. So far he hadn't turned up anything, and that was slightly disconcerting. Her Texas driver's license had come up clean, but he'd gotten nothing else. She didn't have so much as a traffic ticket. The license listed her address as an apartment in Houston, Texas. Rye was going to call the police there and check it out, but first he needed to figure out where she was staying here.

The phone rang again, and Callie went to answer it.

Rye walked to the closet and took out his soon-to-be obsolete Detector 3000. He made sure all the bells and whistles were working. He sighed while he straightened his tie. It was important to present a professional image when dealing with the crazies of the county. The key was to look like he took them seriously.

Callie was slightly breathless. She hung up the phone as Rye walked into the main office. "You might want to hold off heading to Mel's."

"Why?"

She winced. "It appears that Max showed up at the motel with a bunch of roses and was promptly told that Rachel didn't live there. He's been yelling ever since."

"Shit. What's his ETD?" It was Rye's own code. It referred to Max's estimated time of destruction.

"I'd give it about two minutes."

But it was less than that. As the words left Callie's mouth, Max walked by the windows of the sheriff's office. He held a bunch of red roses in one hand, but they'd been through some trauma. Rye whistled as he caught sight of his brother. Big Brother looked like a bull stomping down the street. He plowed through a group of tourists ambling down Main Street.

Rye handed the Detector 3000 to Callie. "Send Logan out when he gets back from dealing with the nudists, naturists, whatever. I've got to go save my brother from himself." Rye jogged out of the office and ran to catch up.

"Hey, buddy, let's talk about this." He would try to reason with Max first.

Max stopped in the middle of the street. Rye took a quick step back, not entirely sure his brother couldn't breathe fire. He looked perfectly capable of it. "There's not a damn thing to talk about. She lied to me."

"She's not staying at the motel. That doesn't mean she's shacked up with someone." He knew exactly what his brother was thinking. Max wouldn't ever consider more innocent options. He was a worst case scenario kind of guy.

"Then why would she lie?" Max's mouth was a stubborn line. He shook his head, clutched his sad-looking bouquet, and started walking toward the diner. His boots thudded along the concrete.

Rye fell into step alongside him. This was a familiar place for Rye. He'd spent a good portion of his life being the voice of reason for Max. Of course, Max played his part, too. Whenever Rye got really mad, Max was the one who watched his back. "You need to calm down. Do you really want her to see this side of you?"

"If she didn't want to see it, she shouldn't have lied." Max's face was set in a mulish stare.

"You're just going to let your freak flag fly, aren't you, bro?" Rye asked more to himself than Max.

Max marched to the diner doors and blew through them like the hurricane he was. Rye sighed. There He had to hope Rachel could handle his brother. He kind of thought she could. Rye didn't bother to follow Max inside. There was nothing he could do now except get in the way. The sight of her beat-up Jeep caught Rye's eye. There was an awful lot of stuff in the back of that Jeep. He had a suspicion and walked over to confirm it.

A few minutes later, he knew his brother was going to feel really bad about yelling at his honey. She was living out of her car. She didn't need Max walking in and announcing her lie to the whole town. She was ashamed.

Sure enough, the doors to the diner opened, and Max stumbled out backward. His eyes were wide and his face registered no small amount of shock as he tripped and landed on his ass. Rachel strode out a second later, roses in one hand. She held them over his head and started to beat the hell out of his brother with them.

Rye fell in love right then and there, and knew there was no going back.

\* \* \* \*

Rachel had been thinking about Max all morning. She couldn't get the previous afternoon out of her mind. She walked around the diner in a pleasant daze, images of Max in her brain.

He'd been everything she could want in a lover.

After they'd gotten out of the pond and dried off, Max had taken a blanket she kept in the back and laid it out under a big cluster of aspen trees. He'd laid her down and spread her legs. Rachel could still feel his mouth on her. He'd parted her labia and gently licked every inch of her slick pussy. Rachel loved the rough feel of his beard on the soft skin of her inner thighs. Her whole body flushed remembering the way he'd fucked her with his tongue.

She felt a slow smile come across her face. Her man might not know it, but she intended to pay him back tonight. She was going to get that big cock of his in her mouth, and she wasn't letting go until she'd blown his mind. Rachel checked the clock. It was almost one. Her shift ended at four, and then she had a couple of hours to get to the motel and check in. She winced at the thought of spending $24.99, but told herself it was just one night. She wanted a night in a real bed with Max. She would get to sleep pressed up against his warm body. The only thing that might be better would be sleeping with Max on one side and Rye on the other.

Rachel shook her head. That wasn't happening. Max had spent a good portion of the previous day talking about his brother. It was obvious they were close. Max had painted a picture of a funny, charming, caring guy who would make someone a good husband. It didn't matter how nice Ryan Harper was, he was a cop, and she didn't want to have anything to do with him. There was too much at stake. Besides, she wasn't that girl. She was a perfectly normal girl on the run from a murderous stalker, and perfectly normal girls didn't get involved with alternative lifestyles.

"I'm telling you, he's up to something," Hank Welch said with a suspicious look in his eyes.

Rachel remembered Hank was the feed store owner. He ran the Bliss County Feed Store Church. He was also a pastor. The feed store portion of his business was closed on Sundays when he held services. He sat across from Teeny Greene, who ran the trading post with her life partner, Marie. Teeny was a little bird of a woman with big brown eyes and a tiny frame. Hank was a small man, but Teeny made him look almost normal.

"I made a mistake and shorted him on his feed. When I offered to fix it, do you know what he said?"

"Probably something you shouldn't repeat." Teeny's eyes were wide as she waited.

Hank took a long drink of his iced tea. "He told me not to worry about it. He said he had plenty for the horses he has right now. He told me I could make up for it with next week's delivery. He's going to kill me, Teeny. I always knew he'd go psycho killer on us one of these days."

"He is not a psycho killer." Rachel was unable to remain silent. She knew exactly who they were talking about. Despite Bliss's odd population, there was only one citizen who everyone believed might go crazy one day. "Max Harper is a reasonable man. He knows you'll make up for the mistake, and that there's no reason to get angry. Anger doesn't solve problems. It just causes more."

Teeny leaned over and whispered something in Hank's ear. The feed store owner smiled broadly. "Are you serious? A dozen?"

She nodded. "He made Marie take all the thorns out so she wouldn't cut herself."

Hank stood up and slapped a twenty down. "Well, that puts a different spin on things."

Rachel was very confused, but picked up the twenty. "I'll get your change."

He shook his head. "None needed, Miss Rachel. You just keep Max happy, and there's more where that came from. You'll have a whole town worshipping the ground you walk on if Max Harper is a happy man." He strode out before Rachel could protest.

Stella walked up behind her and placed a hand on her shoulder. Rachel stared down at the twenty. His bill had been $4.98. She turned to Stella, her mouth hanging slightly open. "Did I just...?" She couldn't quite bring herself to say it.

Stella didn't have the same problem. "I think you just got paid for sleeping with Max. Next time, hold out for more, hon."

Rachel shook her head and stalked over to the cash register. She could feel herself blushing furiously. "How do people know about that?"

Stella laughed loud and long. "This is a small town, Rachel. Get used to it. Everybody is up in everybody else's business."

Teeny grinned. "Besides, Max walked into the store about an hour ago and took all of the roses we got in yesterday. He told Marie we should order in some lilies. He said lilies are your favorite flower."

Rachel flushed. He'd asked her about flowers yesterday. He'd been running a wildflower over her naked breasts at the time. "I do like lilies."

The door to the diner flew open, and Rachel looked up, startled at the sound. Max stood in the doorway, and the expression on his face seemed to mean something to everyone else. He wore jeans and a Western shirt with pearl snaps. His boots had been polished to a shine. His Stetson was shoved on his head, and he didn't bother to take it off. All around her, customers started whispering, and a couple of people dove for cover.

Stella sighed, her eyes rolling. "I'll try to protect the tourists. Hon, now would be a good time for you to run."

Rachel stared at Max, who was glaring right back at her. He targeted her and didn't pay any attention to the rest of the diner. His gorgeous face was locked in an unholy grimace, but she didn't feel a need to run. Rachel had met a truly evil man, and Max just didn't fit the bill. He could growl all he liked. She knew he wouldn't hurt her. He, on the other hand, might not be able to say the same. If she was about to meet the Mr. Hyde part of Max, he'd better get ready to deal with her inner bitch.

"You got a problem with something, Max?" She put one hand on her hip. She didn't know what had happened. She only knew she wasn't backing down.

"You better believe I got a problem, baby," he drawled, but didn't come any closer.

She could see she'd thrown him off by standing her ground. Obviously Max was used to intimidating people. Her heart did a little flip-flop as she wondered if this wasn't Max's way of getting out of the relationship now that he'd gotten what he wanted. He'd seemed so sweet yesterday. He'd been attentive and kind to her even when they weren't making love. She could have sworn he regretted having to leave her for the night. A part of her had started to believe his whole "I'm crazy about you" routine. Maybe it was just a part of Max's game. It wouldn't be the first time a man had lied to get into her pants. She took a deep breath.

She really wished they didn't have an audience. She leaned in to try to keep the conversation between them. "You don't need to make a scene, Max. I get it. It was fun while it lasted. I won't bother you. I'm not some clinging vine. I thought I made it clear to you yesterday. Just make sure you sit in Stella's or Jen's section the next time you come in for lunch." She pointedly pulled out her order form and made her way to table ten. She ignored the angry bull in the room and smiled pleasantly at the couple watching the scene with anxious eyes.

"Is everything all right, ma'am?" The man's eyes kept darting between her and Max.

Rachel waved her hand. "He's just a drama queen. Have you decided on lunch?"

"Drama queen?" Max's shout rang through the little diner.

Rachel sighed. He obviously wanted a big scene. "Excuse me for a minute. If I were you, I'd stay away from the special. Hal isn't really what I'd call a French cook. He just watches a lot of Food Network." She turned back to Max. She didn't try to hide her annoyance. "Is there something I can do for you, Max? Like I said, this scene is unnecessary. All you have to do is tell me you're done. If you have something else to say, make it quick. I have a job to do, and I would prefer to not be fired because my one-night stand turned out to be a big idiot."

His blue eyes were dark. Rachel watched as he clenched his jaw tightly. His words were ground out. "Well, darlin', mine turned out to be a little liar."

Rachel was flummoxed. She quickly went over yesterday's conversation. Most of the time had been spent telling Max how much she loved his tongue and his cock. No lies there. She'd pointedly avoided any talk of her past. "What are you talking about?"

"I just got back from your place, Rach," Max pointed at her like a lawyer in a courtroom drama. "I thought I'd convince Gene to let me into your room and set up a little surprise. Flowers, champagne, the whole romantic treatment. Only no one there's ever heard your name."

Rachel winced inwardly. That explained a lot. She leaned in and lowered her voice. Max might not care about the whole town knowing they were having an affair, but Rachel did. "I was getting a room this afternoon."

"You lied to me."

"What does it matter? I fully intend to be there, Max." Rachel tried to soothe him. She put a hand on his bicep and rubbed. She was pretty sure now that he wasn't trying to break it off with her. "I wasn't trying to trick you."

"I want to know what his name is."

Rachel went cold and dropped her hand from his arm. She took a step back. She couldn't believe this was happening again. "Who are you talking about, Max?"

"Whoever it is you're living with," he said darkly. "Are you married?"

"No." There was a little ember of rage that was always in her belly. Most of the time fear drowned out the rage, but Max was stoking that fire, and Rachel felt her hands start to tremble. "I don't have a boyfriend, either. I thought I might have one, but he turned out to be just another asshole." She stepped forward and pulled the bouquet of roses out of his hand. His face registered shock as she pushed him back. "You're the only man I've slept with in years. I told you that yesterday, but somewhere along the way, I completely forgot you were a man. Men don't believe women."

"Now, Rachel," Max started with obvious trepidation in his voice. He looked like a man whose whole world had just turned over. He backed up, and she continued to push him. His back hit the diner doors.

"I won't put up with it, Max!" Rachel no longer cared that they had an audience. "I won't put up with some possessive asshole who accuses me of cheating every time I'm out of his line of sight."

"I didn't exactly accuse you of cheating." Max muttered something about being wrong just before he tripped and found himself on his ass. His hat came off his head and fell to the side.

It gave Rachel the perfect opportunity to make a few things clear to him. She hit him as hard as she could with the bunch of roses. "You will treat me like a lady, Maxwell Harper. You will politely ask me questions, and you will not accuse me of anything again unless you're damn sure I've done something to deserve it. You will not walk into my place of business and tell the town I'm some sort of harlot. Is that understood?"

Max looked up at her. There were rose petals and greenery in his hair. He looked like he wanted to argue, but he swallowed twice and replied simply, "Yes, baby."

There was a surprised burst of laughter, and Rachel turned to see the Sheriff standing there. He quickly stopped laughing when she turned on him. "Do you want some of this, too?" She held the sad flowers out threateningly.

"No, ma'am," he said.

She glared at him. She'd just whacked the hell out of his brother. He might not take kindly to that sort of behavior. "Are you planning to arrest me?"

"No!" Max shouted.

Rye tipped his hat in a gallant gesture. "Ma'am, anyone can see that your assault of my brother's person was entirely provoked."

"Good." Rachel suddenly felt the weight of the entire diner looking at her. She turned, and, sure enough, there were a whole bunch of faces pressed against the glass. Rachel smoothed her apron down and tossed the bouquet on Max's lap. "I'm going back to work now. You'll understand if I choose not to see you this evening, Max. I've had my fill of men thinking they own me."

"Rachel—" Max got to his feet.

"Goodbye, Max," she said. He looked so sad standing there that she wanted nothing more than to wrap her arms around him and tell him she forgave him. It was a mistake she couldn't afford to make. She forced herself to turn and walk back into the diner. She told herself she could cry over him later.

There was a loud cheer as she walked through the doors and got back to work.

# Chapter Four

Max stared at Rachel's retreating figure and tried to figure out how the hell he was going to fix this. It was obvious now that he'd completely overreacted to the situation. He didn't even understand what the situation was, but he knew he'd done something wrong. No woman had ever tried to brutally kill a man with a bouquet of flowers unless he'd seriously screwed up.

He dusted the rose petals off his shirt and out of his hair. He picked up his hat off the ground and held it in his hand. He would be polite this time. He would follow the rules of courtesy.

"Where do you think you're going?" Rye stood firmly in his way, a barrier to all he held dear.

Max hadn't missed the way his brother looked at Rachel. Rye was falling for her, too, and Max didn't know what to do about it. He couldn't see Rachel accepting the type of relationship they would want. None of that would matter if he couldn't convince her to see him again. "I'm going to talk to Rachel."

The frown on his brother's face let Max know exactly what Rye thought of that plan. "I don't think that's such a good idea, brother. I think she might need a little time to cool down. That honey's downright mean when you get on her bad side."

He was going to have to grovel. He knew it would shock most of the people in town, but he was more than willing to do it if it got him back in Rachel's good graces. "I've got to talk to her."

Rye strode over and put a hand on his shoulder. "She's not going anywhere. If you walk into that diner, you'll be doing the very thing she asked you not to do."

Max let his head fall back in frustration. It was the opposite of the day he'd planned out. He'd bought flowers and champagne. He planned to take her to the Swiss House. It was the nicest restaurant in driving distance from the town. He was going to woo her the way he wanted to. He'd also planned on taking her back to the motel and fucking her brains out, but that was only after he'd made her feel like a princess.

Instead he'd managed to turn his happy kitten into a raging woman scorned because he couldn't control his damn temper. He shoved a hand through his hair and came back with silky rose petals. "I can't leave it like this." He couldn't. It went against his very nature to sit back and hope things turned out okay.

"We have bigger problems, Max." Rye lent him a hand and pulled a long green stem out of the neck of his shirt. "There's a reason she lied about the motel. She's living out of her car."

"What?" Max breathed the question. His mind raced. He thought about the tightly packed Jeep. He'd been too eager to take her again last night. He'd completely missed the signs. Now he remembered that she'd had a blanket in the backseat. It hadn't been neatly folded. It had been laid out and wrinkled up like someone had slept on it. She was sleeping in her car. He'd made love to her, held her, and enjoyed her body and then left her to sleep in her car. Max's heart started to race. Anything could happen to her. There really were bears in the woods, not to mention the fact that anyone could smash in the window and do what they wanted to her.

Rye slapped him on the back. "Calm down. She won't need to sleep in her car anymore. We'll take care of her."

"We have to convince her to move in with us." Max was panicking. How long had she been homeless? What had already happened to her?

"I don't think that's going to be easy." Rye crossed his arms over his chest and appeared lost in thought. "Here's the good news. She isn't intimidated by your temper."

Max laughed. "Hardly." She'd been an avenging goddess coming after him. He'd been intimidated. And strangely aroused.

"The bad news is she now thinks you're a possessive asshole, and she seems to take exception to the type as a whole."

"Well, I am a possessive asshole. At least I am where she's concerned. But hell, Rye, she lied to me. I didn't just make something up this time. I probably should have asked politely, but you know how I get." Rye should know. He was the one who had to talk Max down most of the time.

"I do," Rye said. "If it helps, I don't think it was you she was mad at, not entirely."

"It sure felt like it when she wailing on me." She'd been ready to shove his flowers where the sun didn't shine.

"She said she was tired of men thinking they owned her. If I had to guess, I would say she's had a bad boyfriend or two in her time. Maybe she's been abused. You're going to have to prove you're not just like them."

"Well, I can't go in after her." The whole situation was making Max miserable. All he wanted to do was walk into that diner, throw her over his shoulder, and whisk her away to someplace private. That plan probably wouldn't make Rachel think he was civilized. It would just cement his reputation as a caveman. "She told me not to. If I barge in, I'll be a bullying asshole. If I wait out here for her, I'm a stalker. If I don't wait, she could drive off, and I might never see her again. I need to get her alone and talk to her."

Rye looked back toward the rear lot where Rachel parked her car. "Well, she can't drive off if she doesn't have a car. It would be a damn shame if her car got stolen and taken out to our place. I'd have to wait here to give her a ride over to retrieve her car."

Max thought it was a brilliant idea. His brother was really the devious one. "She didn't say anything about stealing her car."

"Of course, if she decides to press charges, I'll have to arrest you, bro."

"That's a risk I'm willing to take." Max flexed his fingers. He had some work to do. He only hoped Marie had some more flowers left.

\* \* \* \*

By six o'clock, Rachel was dead on her feet. She should have been off two hours before, but she'd let Jen leave early because she could use the cash. She would have worked a complete double if Stella needed the help. She would have done just about anything to avoid the time when she had to drive around and find a place to hole up for the night. Even as she walked through the diner's double doors, tears were threatening to fall.

Why had Max turned out to be a jerk? It was better this way, she told herself. She'd gotten what she wanted out of it. She'd had great sex with a man who knew what he was doing. It was just the sex that she would miss. Max Harper had given her more pleasure than she'd ever had before. She wasn't in love with him, and she didn't want to have anything at all to do with his cop brother.

So why was her heart aching at the thought of not touching him again? She shook her head and sighed. There was nothing to do about it. She wouldn't be involved with a man who treated her like that. He would take and take and give nothing back. She would just put him out of her mind and focus on the problems ahead. She needed a place to sleep. If she found a spot quickly enough, maybe she could read for a while before it got too dark. Then she'd gaze up at the stars and hope to get some sleep.

Rachel stared at the space where her car should be. A horrible panic spread over her body. The spot where she knew she'd parked was empty. Someone had taken her car. It was all she had in the world. All the money she had was in that car, carefully hidden in the floorboard along with her fake IDs and other important papers. She couldn't lose her car.

"Rachel?"

She whirled around, and Rye Harper stood there in his khaki uniform. He looked strangely comforting. "Someone stole my car," she said as she felt tears roll down her cheeks.

Rye shook his head and reached out for her. She was so numb with terror that she allowed him to hold her hands in his. "Rachel, sweetheart, your car is out at the ranch. It's fine."

His words sank in, and her terror turned to anger. Max had done this to her? "He stole my car?"

"Max's youth was…very interesting."

If Max had done the crime, then Rye had to have been in on it. "You let him steal my car?"

Rye's face was open with the faintest hint of a grin on his generous lips. "Well, darlin', I was unfortunately looking the other way at the time. He told me there was a bear coming, and by the time I realized his terrible deception, he was driving off in your Jeep. I think there was some maniacal laughter in there somewhere. Super villains. What are you going to do?"

Rachel didn't appreciate the comedy. She was angrier than she'd been in a long time. She had felt numb for so long, but now the Harper brothers were bringing all her emotions to the surface. "I want him arrested and thrown in jail."

Rye sobered, and then he nodded slowly. "If that's what you want. I'll take you out to our place, and then I'll take him in."

Rachel studied him. "Are you serious?"

He squeezed her hands. She hadn't realized she was still holding his. "Yes, I'm serious. If you want to press charges, then he can spend the night in jail. I told him I would do it when he decided to steal your car."

She sighed, completely confused. He seemed sincere. "Then why would he do it?"

Rye's deep blue eyes held hers. He was so beautiful. Though he looked exactly like his brother, there was a different energy to Rye Harper. He was so much more serene than Max. Max was exciting and wild and made her feel that way, too. Rye made her feel protected.

"Rachel, my brother is crazy about you. He screwed up, and he'll do anything to make it right. Please, just come out to our house and talk to him. If you want me to toss his ass in jail after, then that's what I'll do. I promise."

Damn, but he knew exactly what to say to her. Maybe she was an idiot, but she was inclined to believe what he said. She had to get her car. She supposed she could wait until Stella closed for the night. She could get someone from the diner to drive her out to Max's place, but she found herself walking behind Rye, climbing into the SUV emblazoned with Bliss County Sheriff on the side. She sat beside him with her hands firmly in her lap because she had enjoyed the way his big hand engulfed her small one far too much. She watched the town go by as Rye drove toward his home. She loved the mountains. The small town of Bliss was nestled in the Sangre de Cristo Mountains, and everything about it was magical to Rachel. It seemed so far from Dallas that it could have been on another planet. She could almost believe that she'd run so far no one could ever find her.

"Rachel, why are you living out of your car?"

That brought her right back to reality. She'd hoped they hadn't figured that out. "Is it illegal?"

His sigh told her he was frustrated. "No, I'll drop it."

She looked at the line of his jaw and the weariness of his face. Something softened in her. "I don't have the money to afford a motel," she said quietly, unable to stay silent on the subject.

"It's not safe, sweetheart. Anything could happen to you out here."

He sounded like he really cared. It made her open up a bit. "I know. I don't get much sleep. It's better here in Bliss than some of the places I've been. I feel safer sleeping in the woods than I do in a city."

"I don't suppose you want to tell me what you're running from," Rye continued in a gentle, coaxing voice.

She wasn't willing to go there, certainly not with him. When he found out the man she was running from was a cop, he would take Tommy's side. They all did. She straightened her spine. "Just take me to my car, please."

"All right, Rachel."

They drove the next ten minutes in silence, with Rachel feeling his disappointment sitting between them. There wasn't anything she could do about it. She had her paycheck in her purse and cash stashed in her car. It looked like it was time to leave Bliss. She would get in her car and go to Denver. She'd meant what she'd said to Rye. She felt safer out here, but the city had its advantages. It was easier to get lost in a city. No one noticed new people in big cities.

Rye turned onto a dirt road. Rachel couldn't help being fascinated with the Harper brothers' ranch. It was the most beautiful place she'd ever seen. They passed the pond where she and Max had made love. She could only see a bit of it from the road, but she knew it was there. The road to the house was lined with aspens and wildflowers. She could see the stables and the pasture in the distance. The sun was low in the sky, giving everything a gauzy look. Rye pulled into the long driveway that led to the two-story Victorian manor at the center of everything. Rachel's eyes grew wide. The house looked like something out of a storybook.

"It was our mother's dream house." Rye stared at the big house with a slight smile on his face. Rachel wondered if he was missing his mother. "I've always thought it looked odd out here in the middle of the wilderness. We've tried to keep it up, but I will admit it could use a woman's touch."

There were three rocking chairs on the wide porch, and she saw Quigley lying on the top step. His head came up, and the old mutt wandered down toward the newcomers.

"Hey, boy," Rachel said, putting her hand out. The dog looked very happy to see her. He picked up the nearest stick and tried to press it into her hands.

Rye was laughing a little ruefully. "Naturally. He couldn't stand Nina."

Rachel didn't ask who Nina was. She probably didn't want to know. "Is he in the house?" She could see her Jeep parked next to Max's truck. She bet the keys weren't conveniently in the ignition.

Rye nodded toward the front door. He stood with his knees locked and wariness in his eyes. "Yes. Do you want me to wait around and take him into custody?"

There was no mistaking the anxiousness surrounding him. He seemed to be nervous that she was really going to press charges. She wasn't. Pressing charges wouldn't solve anything. She'd just leave, and then the problem of Maxwell Harper would be solved. "No, Sheriff, I just want my keys."

"All right." Rye let out a relieved breath. He took the stick from Quigley's drooling mouth and tossed it into the wooded area beside the house. The dog loped off after his prize. "I'll just take Q here for a walk so we don't disturb you. Rachel, go easy on him. He's never been in love before. Now that I really think about it, neither one of us has. It's hard. If you're going to leave, please let him down easy." He nodded and walked off after the happily playing dog.

Rachel's heart ached, but she was resolute. She didn't have a place in her life for either of the men. She certainly didn't want to fall in love. She marched up the stairs and knocked on the door.

"Come on in." Max's strong voice rang out.

She took a deep breath, pushed the door open, and stepped into the house. She looked down, and there was a trail of wild flowers leading down the hall. Soft music was playing, and she smelled something truly incredible. Wary, she followed the trail of flowers and found herself in a romantically lit dining room. There were two place settings. Max stood opening a bottle of wine.

"I made you lasagna. You told Jen you liked Italian. It was my mother's recipe. I looked up wines on the Internet. This one is supposed to go with pasta." Max spoke quickly as though he realized he didn't have long to convince her to stay.

"I just want my keys, Max." Her voice was unsteady, as it always was when she blatantly lied. He must have spent all afternoon cooking and getting the house ready for her. She'd been prepared for him to apologize briefly. She'd been ready for him to yell at her. She wasn't ready to find him standing there looking deliciously masculine in a white dress shirt and slacks, preparing to serve her dinner.

He turned his gorgeous face to her. "Rachel, please have dinner with me. I'm so sorry for acting like a dumbass this afternoon. Let me be up front and honest with you. It won't be the last time I make an idiot of myself. I'm really good at it, and I can't seem to help myself. But I promise, every time I do, I'll come groveling and begging you to forgive me."

"I thought you would yell at me for making you look like a fool," Rachel said. He looked anything but a fool to her.

A small smile tugged at his sensual lips. Rachel noted he'd shaved for the occasion. "Darlin', I'm chasing after a woman. I'm only a fool if that woman isn't worth it. You are more than worth every bit of laughter I get hurled my way."

She should leave. She should demand her keys and walk out. The whole scene before her was a romantic trap baited with a hunk of gorgeous man.

He seemed to sense her hesitation. He walked up to her and cupped her shoulders in his strong hands. His blue eyes were kind and very vulnerable as he stared into hers. "I love you, Rachel Swift. I've never said that to a woman before. I love you. Whatever is going on in your life, do not doubt that."

As he leaned down to kiss her, Rachel knew she couldn't leave him. She wondered if she would ever be able to leave him.

He touched his lips softly to hers, and she was lost. She knew what she needed, and at that moment, it wasn't pasta.

"Take off your shirt," she demanded. She wanted his skin against hers.

"Rach?" Max seemed awfully surprised at her commanding tone.

"I said take off your shirt," Rachel repeated. A deliciously wicked thought crossed her mind. He had promised to grovel. "You owe me, mister. I want sexual servitude."

He stared for a moment, and then his shirt hit the floor. Rachel admired his perfectly cut chest. Working with horses had been damn good for his physique. She let her hands roam over the glorious expanse of his chest and down to his abs. She loved the feeling of smooth skin over all that powerful muscle. Tonight he was hers to command.

His smile was a radiant thing. "I am more than willing to be your slave. Consider it my pleasure to do your bidding, baby. Do you want me to eat that sweet pussy of yours? I'll eat until you scream for me to stop."

"Maybe I want to make you scream." She trailed her fingertips across his chest and found the sensitive nipples there. She leaned over to lick one. She was more than happy with his surprised gasp.

"You could definitely make me beg, baby."

She looked up into his clear blue eyes and saw the desire there. It thrilled her that he seemed to want her as much as she wanted him. She pushed herself up on her toes and pressed her lips to his. He stayed still, as though he sensed she needed to be in control for a while. Rachel took his face between her hands and enjoyed the sensual feel of his lips molding to hers. Even on her toes, he had to bend over to kiss her. He was so big. She wrapped her arms around his neck and pressed into his body. She licked along the seam of his lips, requesting entry. He immediately acquiesced, letting her tongue rub against his in a sleek dance.

"Let me touch you," he whispered against her lips.

"All right." She wanted to feel his hands on her, even through the fabric of her jeans and shirt. Max was having none of that. His big hands slid under the waistband of her jeans and cupped the cheeks of her ass. He hauled her up against his body. She could feel his raging erection. It was big and hard and rubbed against her tantalizingly. She knew exactly what he could do with that big, hungry dick, and her pussy started to get slick just thinking about it.

"Tell me what to do, baby," Max practically begged. His body was tense beneath her hands. "It's hard for me to stay still when all I want is to rip these clothes off and sink my cock in."

"You're not very submissive for a love slave." She was surprised he'd lasted this long. He was a very dominant male. It didn't scare her, though. He was tough, but very tender when he made love to her. It was nothing at all like Tommy's assault on her. He'd been ridiculously aggressive on their one date. It had put her off. She shivered in Max's arms.

"Baby?" He pulled her closer, obviously sensing something was wrong.

She shook off the bad memories. She didn't need them. This was Max, not Tommy. He wouldn't hurt her. "Why don't you take these pants off? They seem to be very confining." She cupped his erection through his slacks, and Max groaned.

"You're going to kill me tonight, Rachel." He swore under his breath as his hands went to the zipper of his slacks. He was already sweating as he very carefully lowered the zipper. Rachel practically drooled as he revealed his tapered waist and well-muscled hips. Finally, the full, glorious length of his cock sprung free. It was long and thick, and she could barely get her hand around it. Max gamely kicked off his shoes. He tossed his slacks and boxers to the side. He stood in front of her, naked and thoroughly aroused. Rachel took a seat in one of the dining room chairs and felt a little thrill at her power over this man.

"Rach?" Max's voice was uncertain as she sat back and watched him with utter appreciation for his face and form. He was the most beautiful thing she'd ever seen.

"Tonight is my night, Max," she said with a confident grin. "I'm pretty sure this isn't the last time you'll make an ass of yourself, so I think when you do, you have to cede the sexual power to me. When you make me crazy like you did today, I think I'll just take the reins, and we'll see how you like me torturing you."

"Torture?"

She sighed, sure of the fact that he wasn't going to fight her. He looked slightly nervous, not like a man at the end of his patience. "Yes, Max. You tortured me yesterday. You kissed me until I begged you to fuck me. I cried for it. I think I'd like to return the favor."

All the air seemed to leave his body. "Okay."

"Good." She noticed the heat in the room. It was getting hotter by the second. "Stroke yourself, Max."

His hand cupped his erection. He started at the tip where, Rachel noted with wide eyes, he already had pre-cum dripping from the slit of his cock. He spread the opaque liquid on his palm and stroked from the head to the base. Rachel let out a long breath. His cock was gorgeous. It was big and now had a purple cast to it as his hand glided over and over. The bulbous head gave way to a long shaft with one strong vein running the full length to his tight balls. Rachel wanted to run her tongue along the straining ridge of that vein to feel it pulsing in her mouth. She wanted to cup his balls and feel them tighten, waiting to shoot off.

He continued to pump his cock in his fist, never taking his eyes off her. Rachel wanted to watch him come. This man tore away all her defenses and inhibitions. Somehow, things that would feel dirty or perverse with another man seemed very loving with Max. A forbidden image entered her mind. Rye could be standing beside Max, stroking himself for her pleasure. She would get down on her knees between them and lick those hard cocks in turn.

"Rachel, baby, if you don't stop looking at me like that, I'm gonna come," Max pleaded. He didn't stop what he was doing. If anything, he picked up the pace.

Rachel pulled her shirt over her head and tossed it aside. Her bra, sneakers, and jeans came next. Max watched her with hooded eyes, and Rachel realized he was getting very close to blowing. When she was in nothing but a pair of white cotton undies, she sank to her knees in front of him.

"Max, I want to taste you, and then I want you to come all over my chest. Can you do that for me?" Her mouth was already leaning toward his purple, desperate dick.

"Fuck, yeah." Max replied.

She didn't touch him with anything except the tip of her tongue. She reached out and swiped that delicious salty drop off the slit of his cock, her tongue briefly pushing inside. It seemed to break something in Max.

"Lean back, baby," he ordered, panting as he reached the critical stage.

Rachel leaned back, giving him a perfect target. She watched his beautiful face contort as he started to come. His cheeks flushed and his mouth opened, emitting a long, harsh groan as he covered her breasts with his cum. Rachel felt a rush of satisfaction. He was hers. In that moment, she wasn't thinking about running or hiding or the danger that was still out there. She was in awe of the sensuality she'd discovered and the man who'd shown her how hot she could be. Unselfconsciously, she put on a show for her lover. She rubbed his seed across the soft skin of her chest making sure she coated her nipples with it.

Even though he'd just blown his cum all over her, Rachel saw that his dick was getting hard again.

"God, Rachel, you're so sexy," he breathed, watching her with rapt attention.

Rachel laid back. The hard wood of the floor didn't bother her. She had other things on her mind. Her underwear was soaking wet. "Then you should get down here, Max." She played with her nipples, making sure they were pouty and ripe. "I want you to taste yourself on me."

He fell on her like a starving man. His lips found her nipples, and he quickly sucked the cum off them. He pulled one into his mouth and bit down gently, just to the point of pain. Rachel thought she would come then and there. It was like his mouth had found a path from her nipples to her womb. Her legs moved restlessly beneath him. He lavished attention on her breasts, sucking and biting. While he laved one with his tongue, he pinched the other between his fingers, never letting up on the stimulation.

"Max," she said, unable to take another second, "fuck me."

Max looked up from her chest and smiled. It was the sexiest thing she'd ever seen. "Yes, ma'am."

Rachel pushed her hips up to slide her undies off, but Max had a quicker solution. He reached down and ripped them off her hips. He tossed them aside. He searched out his pants and pulled a condom out of his pocket. He slid it over his cock in one smooth move. Then, to her surprise, he laid back on the floor, offering himself up to her. His cock twitched, already hot and thick again.

"Max?" Now it was her turn to sound unsure.

"I'm here for your pleasure, baby," Max said. "Take me any way you want me. If you want, I'll take over and fuck you senseless, but I thought you might like to be in control."

Rachel straddled his lean hips. She let her hands explore his chest while she settled against him. "You're just about perfect, Maxwell Harper."

He laughed ruefully. "You didn't think that when you were giving me hell, Rach." He reached up to cup her face, and his eyes got very serious. "I love you, Rachel Swift. I'll always give you what you need."

Her heart seized as she realized she loved him, too. God, she was in love. She couldn't say it, though. It was too new and too fragile. All she could do was lean over and kiss him with everything she had.

After a moment, she drew herself back up and guided his rock hard cock to her soaking slit and let gravity do its work.

"You feel so fucking good, baby." He moaned as she lowered herself onto him.

"I love how big you are, Max," she replied, knowing he liked to talk during sex. When he'd made love to her the first time, he kept telling her how hot she was and how much she pleased him. She loved that. "I love how you fill me up." She bit her lip as he did just that. He flexed his hips up and hit that spot deep inside she didn't even realize existed before Max showed it to her.

Max's hands were gripping her hips, guiding her as she rode him. His eyes were on her. She was rapidly discovering Max wasn't a man to close his eyes and enjoy. He wanted to watch.

"And I love the way your tits bounce, baby. It gets me so fucking hot watching you ride me."

Rachel ground her clit on his pelvic bone just as his cock glided over her G-spot. "Oh, God," she moaned as heat and friction exploded from her pussy, coating her entire body with fiery pleasure. She gave herself over to Max's guiding hands as she enjoyed the orgasm blooming across her senses. Max groaned and slammed his hips up one last time. He held her waist tightly as he came.

Rachel fell forward, her head hitting Max's chest. His arms wound protectively around her as their bodies slowly came down from the high of making love. Rachel loved this part, too. She loved the peace she felt as he hugged her to him. There was only one small thing missing, but Rachel refused to think about Rye Harper.

Max chuckled as his hands rubbed across her back soothingly. He was warm, and he made her feel warm, too. "And to think I made you a nice dinner, and all you wanted was sex. I feel so used."

Rachel laughed and snuggled down. "I think we'll get to the food." She kissed his chest and then put her ear over his heart, loving the strong beat. "Eventually."

# Chapter Five

Rye spent the night at Stefan's. Callie was there, and they shared a couple of bottles of wine. He knew what his friends were trying to do. They were trying to get his mind off the fact that his brother was spending the night with the girl of their dreams, and Rye was not.

Late in the evening, after Callie had headed off, Rye sat back in a huge Adirondack chair on Stef's porch and watched the sky. Even though it was summer, it was cool at night. The brisk air felt good, reminding him that there was absolutely nothing to be hot about.

"You know it might not work out," Stef said, taking the seat next to him. He had a light jacket on, but Rye was enjoying the cold.

"I hope for Max's sake that it does." At least Rye wanted to hope that. Damn, he loved his brother. Max was the other half of himself. He should be thrilled that Max had found what he wanted. His fists clenched. A normal brother would feel that way, even if he was attracted to her, too. Of course, a normal brother couldn't sense what his brother was feeling. Max's passion for Rachel was seeping into Rye's blood like a poison. It would ruin him for other women if he let it.

Stef shook his sandy blond head. "It won't, not if it continues this way. Do you think you're the only one who feels the connection between you and Max? I assure you, Max feels it, too. Do you remember how he was when you were in that car accident when we were…how old were we?"

"Seventeen." Rye remembered it like it was yesterday. When he closed his eyes, he could still see the oncoming car, still hear the tires squealing in a desperate attempt to stop what was happening. He still felt the way his heart clenched when he knew nothing would stop the impact. Sometimes his leg still ached from where he'd broken it.

"I was with him when it happened," Stef continued. "No one called us to go to the hospital. We were walking to Callie's to get some notes she took in chemistry, and he stopped and fell to the ground. I thought he was dead. He seemed that way for a good ten minutes. Then he came to, and he couldn't stop crying. He felt you, Rye. He felt you die, and he felt the paramedics shock the life back into you. I don't know or even claim to understand it, but you're more connected than the rest of us. I know I envy the hell out of the both of you."

"Yeah, well the grass is always greener, buddy. It can be hard knowing how someone feels almost all the time. And I can always tell when he wants someone. Usually that's just fine, because he's willing to share. Now that he isn't, I have to wonder how much of what I feel is really me and how much of it is Max."

Stef leaned over. The gravity in his eyes matched the feeling hanging over Rye. "Does it matter?"

That was the million dollar question. Did it matter why a person loved another person? He was pretty damn sure it was love. He'd felt it in little doses before. He'd certainly cared for women before, even enough to think he wanted to marry them. What if what he'd felt before had been small because he'd felt it alone? Max hadn't loved any of the women they had been with before Rachel. He'd liked some of them, wanted most of them, but love hadn't been in Max's vocabulary until Rachel walked into town. What if Rachel was the one?

Rye ran a frustrated hand through his hair. Damn, he was jealous of his brother. And fucking pissed off, too. Max had two weeks with her, to get to know her and let her feel comfortable with him. Where was his equal time? If he'd been the one to meet Rachel first, would he be fucking her right now? He damn straight wouldn't be doing it alone. He'd convince her that they could be good for her, both of them. "He's such a selfish bastard."

Stef laughed a little and leaned back. He let his head rest against the chair and closed his eyes. "He's not and you know it. Max is gruff and obnoxious, but he would give anyone who needed it the shirt off his back. He's just scared."

"Scared? He doesn't seem very scared to me. He seems ridiculously sexually satisfied." Even as he said the words, he knew Stef was right.

"Max is deeper than you like to admit. He's only going to fall in love once. You, on the other hand, could be happy with any number of women."

"Bullshit."

Stef's eyes came open. "I'm serious. If Max weren't around, if you didn't have a twin, you would have gotten married a long time ago and started a family. I'm not saying you would have found the right girl. I'm just saying that you're impatient when it comes to stuff like this. You would have been happy the way most people are. You would have found a restless contentment in your life. Max could never settle for that. Max saved you from that."

Rye wanted to argue. He wanted to point out that he was the mover when it came to their love life. He was the one who made the decisions, but Rye always pulled back in the end because something held him back. It didn't mean as much without Max involved. He knew most people would think it was strange, but it was their love life. Hell, it was their life, and it always had been. He'd accepted it and never really questioned it. He had a second piece of himself, and that was the way it was.

Rye felt weary to his bones. He let the silence stretch between himself and Stef. He remembered back to the night he told Max he wanted to marry Nina. He'd felt Max's panic and now he recognized it for what it was, pain. Max had swallowed his pain at the thought of never finding the woman he could love. He had done it for his brother.

Rye would do it, too. He would stand by and let Max have his love, their love. He would smile and be her friend. Maybe later, he could find that restless contentment Stef had talked about. He could marry and be the best husband and father he could be. He would never let anyone know that he would love his brother's woman to his dying day.

* * * *

"Hey, Rachel!"

Rachel looked over the counter and saw Jen waving at her from the back booth. She grinned and motioned her over. Rachel could see another woman sitting in the booth though her back was to Rachel.

"Go on, hon," Stella said with a nod. "I'll bring your lunch out. You go sit and have some girl talk." Stella's eyebrows went up suggestively. "Maybe you can tell them how you tamed that man of yours last night. He was all sweetness and light when he came in for coffee this morning."

Rachel felt herself flush. She untied her apron and laid it down before walking across the dining room. She couldn't help but think about the night before. They had moved to Max's bedroom after enjoying the lovely dinner he had made. Max had fed her while she sat in his lap, alternating between bites of lasagna and sips of rich wine. Rachel sighed as she remembered. Neither one had worn a stitch of clothing. She'd curled up against him skin to skin, and they'd talked while they ate. It had been the most intimate evening of her entire life. Despite promising to keep all the conversation light, she'd found herself telling him about her childhood, while Max had talked about his brother.

He was so close to Rye. Sometimes he would talk about his brother almost like Rye was the other half of him. She'd never been as close to another person as Max was with his brother. She was an only child, and now her whole family was gone. She knew Max's parents were gone and his sister was off in college, but at least he had his brother.

"Hey." Jen was scooting off the bench when Rachel made it to the booth. "I'm so glad you're going on break. I have to go on the clock. I didn't want to leave Callie in the lurch."

She was leaving? Rachel stared at the woman across from her. She was a pretty woman, roughly the same age as Rachel. Callie Sheppard. She placed a name with the face. She'd seen her around a couple of times, but heard her name almost every day. Callie was the shoulder everyone in Bliss cried on. She was also Rye's administrative assistant.

Callie turned her wide brown eyes up. There was something disarmingly innocent about Callie Sheppard. "I don't like to eat alone. I'm afraid I was running late for my lunch date with Jen. Do you mind?"

Jen bounded away, her ponytail bobbing. Did she mind? Hell yeah, she minded. The last thing she wanted to do was sit down and talk to someone so close to Rye Harper. Everywhere she turned, it seemed Rye Harper was there waiting like a forbidden piece of fruit. She could still feel his hands surrounding hers, even after a full night in his brother's bed. God, what kind of a woman was she?

"Or not," Callie said with a sad twist of her mouth. "It's okay. I can survive one meal by myself."

Rachel slid into the booth. She wasn't about to be rude. She could survive a thirty minute break. "Not at all. I'd love the company."

Stella chose that moment to arrive with Rachel's lunch. It was a very nice turkey sandwich with a bowl of minestrone soup and a glass of iced tea. She greeted Callie with a kiss on the cheek and then left the two alone. Rachel picked up her spoon. "Who wants to eat alone anyway? I'm glad for the company."

Callie sat back and seemed to get lost in thought for a moment. "Would you change your mind if you knew I was here to plead Rye's case?"

The spoon clattered to the table, and Rachel found herself taking a deep drink of her tea. She quickly composed herself. "Rye's case? I don't know what you're talking about. I'm dating Max."

"Yes, that's the problem," Callie replied.

It certainly was. Rachel forced herself to pick up the spoon. She could talk about this, or she could walk away and tell Callie it wasn't any of her business. She knew she should do the latter, but she was so interested in talking about Max and Rye and how they used to conduct their affairs that she found herself staying put. "It's not like it's a grand love affair. Max and I are just having fun." She had to keep it that way.

Callie huffed a little. "Max doesn't have fun. He's serious about you, Rachel. If you aren't serious, it would be better if you broke it off now." Her head tilted slightly to the side. "But I think you're either lying to me or yourself. You're in love with Max."

"After knowing him a few weeks? I hardly think so." Rachel kept her tone nonchalant.

A sad smile crossed Callie's face. "You don't believe in love at first sight?"

Callie did. Rachel could see that plainly. She softened a little. From everything she understood about the other woman, she was probably lonely. Bliss was a small town. There probably hadn't been many prospects. From the stories Rachel had heard, Callie had been the only girl her age. She'd grown up with the Harper twins and Stef as her only real companions. They had been kids and then teens together. With so few suitable males her age, Callie had probably fallen in love with one of her friends. She couldn't see Callie with the artist, so that left Max and Rye. Rachel's heart ached a little. Callie wasn't doing the whole "stay away from my men" business. She was watching out for two men she loved.

"I'm not trying to hurt anyone." Rachel watched as the other woman looked away.

"I know. I just don't think you understand them." Callie took a long drink of her coffee. The salad in front of her went untouched. "I know it seems weird, but two men can be really nice."

Now Rachel was the one leaning in. "Did you date them?"

Callie's eyes widened. "God, no. I wasn't talking about them. Look, I grew up with them. I'll admit that when I was a kid I had a crush on them, but really, I'm over that. I love them, but I'm not in love with them anymore. Now they're like my obnoxious brothers. My question is, are you even vaguely attracted to Rye?"

Was she attracted to Rye? Yes, but she shouldn't be. She thought about the way it had felt to sit next to him in the truck the night before. His very presence had pulled at her. She'd wanted so badly to scoot over and sit next to him, their hips brushing each other as the Bronco bounced down the road. It was different than what she felt with Max. Despite her every instinct telling her to stay as far away from Rye Harper as she could, she couldn't get the image of him standing over her out of her head. Max, for all his bluster, was sweet and so tender when it came to sex. Rye would be a different story.

"Okay, that answers that question," Callie said. She had a big grin on her face, and Rachel felt herself flush. She'd given away way more than she thought she had.

"Fine, I find him attractive. That doesn't mean I'm going to jump his bones." She wasn't going to do that. Even if she wanted to, it would hurt Max. She wasn't going to cheat on Max.

"Are you fundamentally opposed to the whole idea of a threesome?"

Again, Rachel felt every inch of her face flood with blood. She looked around to see if anyone was watching. "How can you talk about this?" Something Callie had said earlier suddenly made sense. "You're in a threesome, aren't you?"

Finally, Callie showed some discomfort with the very intimate subject. Her hands twisted together. "No, not on a permanent basis. I mean, wow, that makes it sound like I'm going to an orgy every weekend. I'm not. My life would be way more interesting if that was happening." She stuttered a little. "I only did it the once, but that was enough."

"Enough for what?"

"Enough to make me think about it for the rest of my life." Callie took a deep breath and visibly forced her hands to be still. "It was one weekend with two amazing men. At the end of the weekend, we went our separate ways. I haven't seen them in years now. They were friends of Stef's."

But Callie hadn't wanted the weekend to end, Rachel knew suddenly. It was written all over her face. Rachel felt a rush of empathy for Rye's assistant. "What was it like?"

Rachel wasn't necessarily talking about the sex, and Callie seemed to understand. A dreamy look came over her face. "I've never felt safer than I did with them. It was like I was their whole world. When I was with Zane and Nate, I was something more than just me. Maybe it works that way with just couples, but I was surrounded by them. I was the center of the whole world for a little while. I wouldn't trade it for anything."

"But your heart got broken." And that was what Rachel was terrified of.

Callie shrugged and shook off the fine sheen of moisture that coated her eyes. "You can't make someone love you. I wouldn't take back loving them, either. Loving makes us better. And you won't have the same problem. Max is already in love with you. Rye can't help but follow. It just works that way for them."

"Always?"

Callie nodded. She seemed more comfortable getting back to the subject of Max and Rye. "Ever since we were kids. You know that connection thing a lot of twins have? Multiply it by a thousand, and that's Max and Rye. I swear one can tell what the other one is thinking most of the time. When they started dating, they dated the same girl. At the same time. And then her father came after them with a shotgun, and they ran away together."

Rachel felt a smile split her face. What must it be like to have someone to share your soul with? How hard would it be to suddenly stop? She frowned. "Max hasn't broached the subject with me. I don't think he wants to share me." And she wasn't about to suggest a threesome. Even if she wanted to. Which she didn't.

"I think he's afraid of scaring you off. They're both afraid of scaring you off. If you really care about Max, please think about giving Rye a shot. He's a great guy."

All thoughts of food were put on hold. What was she doing? She couldn't stay here, could she? She couldn't think about giving a relationship with a sheriff an honest try. He didn't even know her real name.

"I mean he's paranoid," Callie was saying. "But you're good. You passed the background check. Once your plates clear, and he's sure you're not a serial killer, you'll find him to be the nicest guy ever. Of course, Mel might still think you're an alien, but I have a test for that, too."

Callie continued, but Rachel's vision had shifted. Everything was a little blurry as she realized Rye Harper had already proven her point. She couldn't trust him. God, what did he already know? Had he called around? Her current license listed her address as Houston, but cops shared info all the time. Was Tommy already on his way?

Rachel stood up, ignoring Callie's surprised look. She walked to the counter and picked up her keys. Stella called out, but Rachel didn't respond. She walked out the door and got into the Jeep. She would leave. No goodbyes, no last paychecks. She would point her Jeep to the north and head for Wyoming. She would drive past Denver because it was too close to the Harper twins for comfort. She would dump the Rachel Swift ID. When she had enough cash, she would make her way to Chicago and lose herself in the city. She wouldn't make friends. She wouldn't talk to anyone unless she had to. She sure as hell wouldn't fall for another man. She turned the car around. She felt tears running down her face. How could he have done that to her?

She stopped at the red light. Something made her turn her head. She wanted one last look at Bliss. And then she saw him. Rye Harper was walking out of the sheriff's office. He stretched and yawned, pulling his big body this way and that way. His eyes caught sight of her and lit up. There was a wide smile on his too sexy mouth, and his hand came up in greeting.

Suddenly, she just had to wipe that smile off his face. Jerking the car into park and pulling the keys out, Rachel opened the door and descended on the man who had just wrecked her life.

# Chapter Six

Rye yawned as he walked into the sunshine. It was turning out to be a lazy day. No alien invasions. No complaints from the tourists about naked hikers. No bombs going off on the Farley land from out of control science experiments. It was a good thing, too, because he had a headache from drowning his sorrows the previous night. His stomach growled. A burger from Stella's was what he needed. A little grease and his stomach would settle right down. If he hurried, he could catch up with Callie.

Rye turned as a battered Jeep stopped at the stop light in front of his office. He caught sight of Rachel's strawberry blonde hair pulled into a ponytail. His breath hitched at the sight of her. God damn, he cursed inwardly, even as he felt a dippy smile cross his face. It was like she was the freaking sun. He felt his hand come up to wave at her.

She slammed her car door shut. She was wearing a tight white T-shirt and jeans that hugged her every curve. Her breasts were gloriously round and jiggled as she walked toward him. Her hips swayed. His hands itched to walk straight up to her and drag that hot body against his. He would grind his erection against her and force her to come at least twice before he shoved her over and shoved his cock inside. He would ride that pussy until he finally couldn't take another second and then...oh, then, he would come. He would flood her with every last drop he had in his balls.

Damn it, he had an erection right in the middle of the street, and now he had to talk to her. Rye finally got a good look at Rachel's face and took a step back. She looked righteously pissed, and all that anger seemed to be directed at him.

"You asshole!" She stalked across the distance between them.

Her anger practically vibrated through the air. Rye knew he should ask what was wrong, but something about the way she was coming at him got his back up. Not just his back, his cock was straining, too. She wanted to fight. He could fucking fight. He hadn't done anything but facilitate her relationship with his brother and offer her his protection. He wasn't about to take her shit.

"You want to move that car, Ms. Swift?" He crossed his arms over his chest and gave her his best lawman stare.

It made her stop in her tracks, but only briefly. "What are you going to do, Sheriff? Give me a ticket? Lock me up?"

He could think of a few things he would do. None of them had anything to do with jail. "Maybe I'll just spank that ass of yours, sweetheart."

He shouldn't have said it, but the words were out of his mouth before he could think twice. It was exactly what he'd do if she was his woman. If she belonged to him and she'd pulled this shit, he would lay her out over his knee, and she wouldn't get up again until she'd nicely apologized.

"What did you say?" She practically growled the question at him. Her eyes narrowed, and she held her ground.

Rye towered over her. "I said I would spank that little ass of yours red, darlin'."

"I think Max might have something to say about that." She shot the words at him, but there was a telltale trembling to her voice. He would bet everything he had that she wasn't entirely put off by the prospect of getting over his knee.

Max would watch if their relationship was on a normal footing. For all his anger issues, Max was softer than Rye when it came to sex. It didn't mean Max didn't enjoy playing a few games. He'd spanked a perky little ass on more than one occasion. "You push Max like you're pushing me, and he'll understand."

Her eyes flared briefly before she hardened them to flinty green stones. "Yeah, well, you don't have to worry about it. I'm leaving. Don't worry about me screwing up your perfect world anymore."

She started to turn, and Rye's arm shot out. He was running on pure emotion. She was leaving? Not on his watch. "Where the hell do you think you're going?"

She pulled against him, setting her sneakers solidly against the road. "It's none of your fucking business, Sheriff. Let me go."

Not on his life. Rye looked around and realized they were stopping traffic. Rachel's car could wait. He needed to figure out what the hell had turned her into a raging maniac, and he couldn't do it in public. Without letting go of her arm, he leaned down and slid his free arm beneath her leg. He hauled her up against his chest and strode back toward the sheriff's office. No one was in there. They could yell at each other in perfect privacy.

He kicked the door open and walked her back to the small confines of his office. He set her down and swiftly blocked the door. "Now, do you want to be reasonable about this, or should I get ready to administer a little discipline?"

Her face was red, and her small hands were clenched into fists at her sides. "You let me go right now, or I swear I will sue you for everything you're worth."

"Feel free," Rye shot back. "Take me for everything I'm worth. You're not leaving."

"You can't keep me, asshole."

"Watch me." He leaned back against the door. "And watch your language, Rachel. You curse me one more time, and I won't give a damn that you belong to Max. I will pull those jeans down and leave an imprint of my hand on your ass."

"You're a big man to threaten a woman, aren't you?"

Rye laughed. "Yeah, poor little Rachel. You're so downtrodden." Tears filled her eyes, and Rye practically melted. He took a step toward her, his hands curving over her shoulders. "Baby, I didn't mean it. I wouldn't hurt you. It's a game. Fuck, I'm sorry. Please tell me why you want to leave. I promise I'll make it all right." All of his anger evaporated like someone had taken a pin to a balloon, popping it, deflating him. He couldn't help himself. He pulled her into his arms.

"I'm sorry." He was willing to say anything to make her stop crying.

Her hands came up across her chest as though she couldn't stand to be so close to him. He would call Max. She only wanted Max. His heart hurt. And then her arms wound around his waist, and she sobbed into his chest. A great sigh of relief left Rye's lungs. He let his head sink down against her hair. His hands soothed over her back. "I'm sorry." He said it over and over. He wasn't even sure who he was saying it to. He was sorry something bad had happened to her. He was sorry he'd done something to piss her off. He was so, so sorry she wasn't his. He wanted nothing more than to call Max and take her home where they could take care of her. She would be their princess, their partner, their perfect lover. God, he was so sorry she didn't want that.

After a long while her head came up, and she pulled away slightly. "I apologize for yelling at you, Sheriff."

A veil had come down over her eyes. Rye's chest constricted. She was shutting down the intimacy between them. It was good one of them had a lick of sense, but he wished she was still in his arms. "Please tell me what's wrong."

She shook her head. "It's best I just leave."

"Baby…Rachel, I know something's wrong. I'm not stupid. I also know none of it's your fault."

"How can you possibly know that?"

He sighed and brushed back a piece of hair that had fallen out of her previously perfect ponytail. "I just know. And even if it was your fault, I would take care of it." He cleared his throat. "You're my brother's girl. I would take care of you. If someone's after you, I'll move heaven and earth to stop him. If you got caught up in something bad, I'll take care of that, too."

Her face contorted and, for a moment, he worried she would start crying all over again. Then she shook it off, and that wall of mulish strength she had came down between them. "No, I'm fine. But stay out of my business."

Shit, she had found out about the trace he'd run on her. *Damn Callie's big mouth.* And Rachel's reaction did nothing but make him even more suspicious. "I don't know if I can do that, Rachel."

Her chin came up stubbornly. "All right. Then I'm leaving, and there's nothing you can do. Unless you intend to put me in jail, I suggest you let me move on."

He wanted to punch something. His gut rolled with anger, need. He wasn't sure what he was feeling anymore. "God damn it, Rachel. You really want to put me in a corner, don't you? I know something's wrong, but if I pursue it, you'll leave, and then my brother will hate the very sight of me."

Her shoulders slumped. "It would be best if I left, Rye. I'll let Max know you didn't have anything to do with it."

He forced her chin up to look into those green eyes. He couldn't help but touch her. "Don't go. I'll stop looking. I'll leave it alone. I promise." He wouldn't promise not to protect her. He wouldn't promise not to come between her and anything that came her way.

Her lips trembled. They were close. All he had to do was lean down, and he could press his mouth to hers.

There was a loud bang as the door to the station house opened.

"Hey, Bro, you here?" Max's voice rang through the building.

Rye and Rachel jumped apart like there was a blazing fire between them. Rachel's back was against the wall when Max opened the door to the office. "Hey, what's Rachel's Jeep doing parked in front of a stop light?" Max's face lit up when he saw Rachel. "Hey, baby."

Rachel shouldered her way past both of them. "Your brother's an asshole. I have to go back to work."

Max watched her stalk out. There was a dippy grin on his face when he looked back at Rye. "Damn, you pissed her off but good. Glad it wasn't me for a change. She should watch that language, though. I just had the most insane urge to spank her. You want to go get lunch?"

It took everything he had not to scream. "Yeah, sure. Anywhere but Stella's. I don't think I would like what Rachel would do to my food." Rye forced himself to follow his brother out the door.

# Chapter Seven

Rachel woke up smiling. There were lines of early morning sunlight cascading through the curtains. Rachel turned over and reached out for Max.

The last week had been damn near perfect. Since her near miss with Rye in his office, she'd managed to avoid him for the most part. She'd spent her days working and her nights with Max. Rye had worked the night shift or stayed with friends. She knew Max missed him, but it was for the best. It was still a worry in the back of her mind that she was coming between them, but she wasn't sure how to fix it. Max seemed so happy. Rachel had decided, for once in her life, to live in the moment. Everything went bad eventually. She should enjoy Max while she could.

Rachel rubbed her eyes and sat up as she realized she was all alone in the huge bed. She could hear the water running in the bathroom and stretched languorously, deciding Max must be in the shower. Every muscle hummed with satisfaction as she really looked around the bedroom. They hadn't spent much time in the big bedroom. There were five bedrooms in the house. Both Max and Rye had their own bedrooms, and, until last night, she and Max had stayed in his room. Max had made the decision to move them into the big bedroom the night before. He'd been very serious when he told her to get her stuff, as though moving into this room meant something to him.

The bed was enormous. It had to have been custom-made. It was bigger and longer than a king and would easily fit three people. She sat up and got out of bed to look around. The large dresser across from the bed was very telling. There was a small dish where Max placed his keys and his watch. There was a second, matching dish that was empty on the other side of the dresser, and in the middle, an empty jewelry box. Rye and Max had shared this room with a woman at least once. She remembered someone mentioning a woman named Nina. Rachel wondered how long she'd stayed with the brothers as their shared woman. She tried to imagine what would cause a woman to leave.

The dresser seemed sad and lonely with just Max's watch and keys sitting there. She wondered where Rye had spent the previous evening. She'd heard him come in after midnight, but he'd made himself scarce. He'd given them space for the last several days, just as he'd said he would.

Rachel shook off unsettling thoughts of her boyfriend's twin brother. Grinning, she realized that Max really was her boyfriend. She couldn't deny it. A woman didn't get intimate and emotional over a short-term affair or a booty call. The mirror in front of her revealed something shocking. There was a lovely woman in the glass, and she was practically glowing. She wasn't scared or worried. She just looked well loved.

She looked like a woman who knew what she wanted. Rachel winked at the woman she barely recognized as herself and decided that it was time to go get what she wanted. Without bothering with her clothes, she strode into the bathroom. It was a gorgeous monstrosity. There were three sinks before the long mirror and an oversized jetted tub, but what caught her attention was the man in the large glass shower. The heat from the water had steamed up the entire bathroom, but she could see his shadowy form through the opaque glass. It didn't matter that she couldn't see him clearly. She'd memorized every inch of that hot body of his, from his broad shoulders to his strong legs. Now it was time to greet the day properly, Rachel thought, her body heating up.

She quietly opened the shower door and slid in behind Max. He was facing away from her, his arms carefully soaping his muscular body. Rachel took in the sight of his toned backside for a moment before cuddling up behind him. She pressed her breasts against his back and wound her arms around his waist.

"Good morning, gorgeous." She let her hands wander down. She grasped his cock and was not surprised to discover it was already hard and long. It seemed to be his permanent state. "Is this for me?"

"God, yes," he said.

His cock swelled in her hand, and she could feel the heat in his skin.

"Rachel," he groaned as she stroked him from bulb to base.

"Hush, let me take care of you this morning," she whispered, trailing little kisses along his strong spine. She let her tongue find his skin. She loved the taste of him. "You took care of me last night."

He had. Four times. She fully intended to pay him back, with interest. She had hours and hours until she was due at the diner. There was no reason at all they couldn't spend those hours in bed.

Max's hand went out to steady himself against the wall of the shower. "Rachel, you have to stop."

"Not until I get what I want." Rachel slowly cupped his balls. "I'm going to put my mouth on you. I'm going to suck your cock until that moment just before you explode, and then I'm going to bend over and let you fuck me from behind."

"Rachel, please stop." There was a desperate quality to his voice.

She felt his cock pulse in her hands. "Not on your life, Max."

"I'm Rye," he choked out.

Rachel nearly fell over as she jumped away from him.

Rye turned and steadied her. "I'm so sorry, sweetheart. You were asleep, and there's no hot water in the guest room. Max is out in the pasture working with some of the horses."

Rachel stumbled out of the shower, looking for a towel. She hit the marble of the floor and quickly found herself on her ass.

Rye rushed to help her. He reached out and pulled her up. "Are you okay?"

She closed her eyes. "No, I'm not. You're naked."

"It's how I shower," Rye explained academically.

She opened one eye. He was so gorgeous. His broad shoulders gave way to a lean, ripped chest and a six-pack that made her mouth water. "And do you always shower with a raging hard-on?" He'd been rock hard before she'd gotten her hands around him. She knew just from the feel of him that he and Max were perfectly identical twins.

He shrugged and blushed. "Lately, yeah."

Rachel caught him looking down at her breasts. "Stop."

He looked away. "I'm sorry, Rachel. You're just so fucking beautiful, I can't help it. I'll get you a towel." He turned and treated Rachel to a view of his perfect ass. It was just lovely. He grabbed a big white towel and wrapped it around her. "I'm sorry."

She backed up. "You keep saying that, Rye, but you're still naked." She pulled the towel around her and stalked back out into the bedroom so she would stop ogling her boyfriend's brother.

Rye followed. "Well, you took my towel."

But he already had another one in his hands, and he wrapped it around his lean waist. Rachel shook her head. Covering up didn't make him any less delicious. Rachel looked around the room for her clothes. She opened a drawer and pulled out a T-shirt. She thought it must be Max's. The dresser was loaded with T-shirts and sweatpants.

"You should have told me who you were the minute I stepped into the shower with you," Rachel complained, shoving the blue T-shirt over her head.

Rye ran a frustrated hand through his wet hair. It was so much longer wet. "I couldn't breathe enough to talk, Rachel. I'm so sorry. I should have locked the door. I should have just skipped the damn shower. Hell, I should have spent the night somewhere else. I knew something like this would happen."

Rachel was confused. She calmed down as she noticed Rye looked a little tormented. "Rye, we didn't do anything we shouldn't have. It was a mistake. I'm sure this isn't the first time a woman got twin brothers confused and ended up seeing more than she should. It's your house. I'm the one who should be more careful."

Rye turned away from her. He placed both hands on the dresser. His head fell forward as though he was very tired. "We've shared a room all of our lives until a year ago. Even after our parents were gone and we could have, probably should have, taken our own rooms, we didn't. We just moved in here and, when we had the money, renovated to suit our needs. We built this room and that bathroom for the future. I don't know, Rachel. I just always expected him to be there."

"I am not trying to take your brother away from you," Rachel said quietly. She wondered if all the drama was worth it. Her heart hurt a little at the thought, but sooner or later, she would have to move on. Until Tommy was caught, she was in danger and so was everyone around her.

Rye sighed. "Oh, Rachel, I'm not jealous of you." He turned to her, and the intensity in his blue eyes made her heart speed up. "I'm gut-churningly jealous of Max. All of our lives, I've been the one to find our women. He's a charmless bastard who just went along for the ride. I'm the one who wanted to get married. I'm the one who wanted to have kids. He just wanted to fuck. Now, he's the one who finds you? How the hell is that fair?"

Rachel stood there, watching him at war with himself. She wanted to wrap her arms around him and soothe him, but she didn't have the right. From everything she knew, Max had decided to go straight. He wanted a normal one-on-one relationship. He would probably be very upset if he knew how attracted she was to Rye.

Rye just shook his head. "I'm leaving tonight. I'll pack a couple of things and stay at Stefan's until I can find an apartment."

"Don't." Rachel was horrified at the thought. "I'll leave. This is your home. I never meant to cause so much trouble."

Rye smiled slightly, but it was a sad thing. "I can't watch you and Max, Rachel. I'll get to the point where I can be friendly, and we can pretend to be some sort of normal family, but I'll never stop wanting you. I can't live in the same house and watch you settle in with my brother. Do you understand the relationship I want?"

Rachel nodded. "You want to share me with Max." The statement came out in a low, breathy voice. She had meant to sound matter-of-fact, not sultry.

"I want you between us, Rachel. I want you to be our wife and our lover and the mother of our children. I want you to sleep in between us. I want you screaming your pleasure when we take you at the same time. Do you understand?"

"Yes, I understand." Her mouth was dry as she thought about it. She could have both of them. Two gorgeous men, loving her, wanting her. It was the fantasy of a lifetime.

"Max doesn't want that anymore. I have to choose between pursuing the woman I think I was meant to be with and honoring the brother I've shared a life with from the moment we were conceived. Know this, Rach, if he weren't already madly in love with you, if you hadn't already chosen him, I would be all over you. That's why I have to leave."

"Rye," she started, but couldn't think of anything else to say.

He turned. His chest was still slick from the shower. "And change, Rachel. That's my shirt. Max won't like you running around in my shirt. He keeps his extra T-shirts on the right side of the dresser."

He started to leave, but all of a sudden, he stumbled. His knees hit the wood of the floor, and he gasped. Rachel hurried to his side to try to help him up. He was shaking. His hands trembled slightly as he held his head.

"It's Max," he said in obvious distress. "Oh God, Rachel, he's hurt."

\* \* \* \*

Max breathed in the early morning air, aware of a sense of contentment he'd never felt before. Rachel was still asleep in their bed. Her sweet, soft body was curled up under the quilts. He'd slept wrapped around that body. Their arms and legs had tangled in the night, and when he woke up, her hair was all over his face. He'd grinned and managed to find his way out of the web her strawberry blonde hair had woven around him. He'd watched her sleep for a while, then rose quietly to get his work for the morning done.

He had to pay attention to work. Before he'd met Rachel, work had been all that mattered. Now he had to tell himself to get his ass up. He had to make some money since he had a woman to support now. Rachel might not know it, but she was his top priority. He would get her comfortable living with him and then move her gently toward marriage.

Max made sure the saddle on Maverick was cinched tight, then mounted with the ease of a true horseman. The big horse beneath him nickered and waited for a command. Now that the morning's maintenance was done, it was time for some exercise. The stall for Sunflower was ready. She would be arriving tomorrow, and Max was eager to get to work with her. For now, he would settle for riding the pasture and making sure the fences were solid.

Quigley followed the quarter horse as Max let Maverick trot out of the yard toward the big pasture where he'd be able to gallop. Max's mind wandered as they made their way down the road.

He wanted to marry Rachel, but there was one thing marring the vision. It was hard for him to think of marrying a woman without his brother at his side. He knew Rye was attracted to Rachel, probably at least half in love with her. They had always wanted the same women. Perhaps, if they had grown up in a more conventional town, they would have been shamed into giving up their instincts. Everything in

Max told him to share with his brother. They were happier that way. If they had been told how wrong and perverse they were, maybe they would have been able to deny that part of themselves.

But they had grown up in Bliss. Their mother had accepted them, and their father had been far too busy drinking to care what they did. The town itself was so full of hippies and free spirits that when Max and Rye asked one girl to be their date to the winter festival when they were sixteen, everyone had smiled indulgently and talked about how comfortable the boys were in their own skins.

Rachel hadn't grown up in Bliss. Rachel had grown up in suburban Texas, according to her stories from childhood. She'd been raised conventionally, and she would probably walk out if he even suggested that they experiment. She would be shocked if she knew what he really wanted.

She wasn't some girl Rye had picked up in a bar who wanted to have some fun and play out a few fantasies. Max had enjoyed the long-term relationships they'd had with women like that, but, unlike his brother, he'd known those relationships wouldn't end in happily ever after. Max was more cynical than Rye. He knew there wasn't a woman out there who wanted to put up with two men. They were too demanding.

It wasn't like they hadn't had sex separately before. They had both had many relationships that didn't involve the other brother. It was just anything even vaguely serious had been a ménage. When Rye had really fallen for someone, Max had inevitably fallen a little, too.

Max thought about how tired Rye had looked this morning. He'd been up and drinking coffee when Max had come through the kitchen. Their conversation had been polite, but there was a distance between them that put Max on edge.

"You look like hell, brother," Max said, pouring coffee into his thermos. "Late night?"

Rye shook his head. He was wearing a pair of sweats and his running shoes. Max knew that Rye ran off his problems. He would run for miles when he was upset. From the sweat covering his brother's body, Max knew he'd been running all morning. "It was fine, but I think I'll take off for a few days. Stef wants to go fishing before the Founder's Day picnic."

Max turned and studied his brother. "I don't want to run you off. I want you to be okay with Rachel staying here."

Rye's laugh was short and sharp. "I'm okay with it. I just think the two of you need some time to yourselves, and then we need to figure some stuff out."

Max found himself getting upset. He could sense Rye's anxiety. "Figure out what?"

Rye looked frustrated as he dumped his coffee in the sink. "Well, I'm not going to be your and Rachel's roommate. Do you really think I want to watch that? Do you think that's how I want to spend the rest of my life?"

"Ryan," Max said, trying to stop his brother.

"Don't." Rye put a hand out to stop him. "I'm happy for you, man. I really am. I just isn't what I thought our lives would be like, and I need time to adjust. We'll figure it all out in the end. Besides, you can't really want me around. I make Rachel nervous."

"She'll get used to you." Max needed to believe that.

"No, she won't," Rye replied sadly. "She's not that girl, and maybe we were fooling ourselves. I can see now that Nina was never going to make both of us happy. Hell, she wouldn't have made me happy. I proposed to her because I wanted to get married. She said yes because she didn't have anything better to do. It was stupid. Rachel is the type of girl you marry and raise a family with, and she's also the type who would never accept a ménage."

"Come on, Rye." He couldn't think of anything else. Rye wasn't saying anything he hadn't thought of already.

"I'm going to take a shower. I'll see you later," Rye said in a voice that told Max he was done for now. Then Rye had disappeared down the hall, and Max had gotten to work.

Max tried to put his brother out of his mind as he turned Maverick down the short slope marking the change between yard and pasture. He could already see a place in the fence that he needed to fix. He would have to figure out how to fix the mess with his brother at a later date.

Max heard a sound like a car backfiring. For the briefest of moments, he felt his anger flare. Someone was up at the house at this time of the morning? It was Saturday. Couldn't they be left in peace on a Saturday morning?

Then he felt the pain bloom along his left arm. He looked down. There was blood starting to spread on his shirt.

*I've been shot,* Max realized with shock.

It had finally happened. Some damn hunter had let a bullet go wild.

Max turned Maverick, who was antsy now, and started to move toward the woods. He would show that hunter a thing or two. Damn asshole probably didn't even realize he'd hit someone.

The sound came again, and Maverick bucked wildly. Max had to pull hard on the reins and hunker down to stay on the horse. There was a third shot. Maverick took off as he completely panicked. Max was thrown to the side. His own panic set in as he realized his boot was stuck in the stirrup. He tried to pull free as he was dragged along the ground, but he couldn't make it.

Max heard Quigley barking frantically. The dog raced to keep up with his master. Max gave his boot one last tug and then felt his head hit something hard. The whole world went black.

* * * *

Rachel didn't stop to think when Rye made the announcement that Max was hurt. She ran. She ran out the door and down the porch steps. She didn't think about the fact that she was barefoot with only Rye's T-shirt to cover her. All she could think about was Max. She suddenly knew that Rye was right, and he needed them.

"The stables." Rye ran up behind her. He pointed behind the house and started sprinting.

He was barefoot, too, Rachel noted, but had slipped into sweatpants. He raced toward the back of the house. As Rachel followed, she saw something that terrified her.

Maverick was standing perfectly still in the yard. He looked down at Max, who was on the ground. His booted foot was still in the stirrup, and his big body was completely still. Quigley danced around him anxiously. The enormous dog whined.

Rachel's heart seized. Rye made it to his brother's side and felt for a pulse. Rachel got to her knees, reaching out for his still hand.

"Call an ambulance," Rye said urgently.

She needed to touch him, to hold him, to assure herself that he was alive.

"Rachel, call 911 now!" Rye's voice broke through her fear.

Rachel raced back to the house and called. Every second she prayed she hadn't seen him alive for the last time.

# Chapter Eight

The next several hours were the worst of Rachel's life. She and Rye sat out in the waiting room of the hospital in Del Norte while Max was in surgery. The doctor told them he'd been hit by two stray bullets. It wasn't an uncommon occurrence. There was a hunting rifle slug in his left arm and another in his leg. That was the easy part. The bullets hadn't hit any major organs. His brain, on the other hand, had taken a beating. He had a concussion, and they weren't sure about the severity of it.

By the time Rye and Rachel reached the hospital, several of the brothers' friends and family members were already on their way. Within minutes of speaking to the nurses and settling in to wait, Rachel heard someone call out Rye's name. Callie Sheppard and Stefan Talbot rushed in and immediately assaulted Rye with questions.

Rye had calmed everyone down by the time the doctor came out to explain that Max's head trauma wasn't as bad as they'd first believed. He was still in surgery for the bullet wounds and would need to stay in the hospital overnight, but the doctors were sure he would pull through.

"Which one of you is Rachel?" The doctor looked at the two women in the group with an amused smile on his face.

Rachel held up her hand, feeling very self-conscious. "That's me."

The doctor grinned. "Well, Mr. Harper came to while we were taking the CT scan. He's not a pleasant man."

Stefan and Rye laughed.

"He was insistent about seeing you, young lady," the doctor said. "We had to promise that you would be in his ICU room when he came out of surgery. He was very difficult."

"I can imagine." Rye's shoulders, which had been bunched around his neck for hours, finally settled into a more normal position. "You really won't want to keep him here more than a day."

Rachel could feel him calming down now that he knew his brother was out of real danger. If Max was bitching, then he was okay.

"They could sedate him," Stefan said helpfully. Rachel looked at the handsome artist. From what Stella had told her, he was very famous and very reclusive. He was quiet every time he came into the diner. This was the first time Rachel could remember seeing him smile.

"They would have to," Callie remarked. Rye's admin looked very comfortable with the two men, each of whom had a foot and a hundred pounds on her.

"He's all right, then?" a soft voice asked. Rachel turned around to see a gorgeous brunette with large blue eyes looking at the little crowd. She was stark white, as though all the blood had left her body, and there was a sheen of tears coating her eyes.

"Yes." Rye's face lit up, and he opened his arms. The young woman rushed into them. He wrapped her in a bear hug, kissing the top of her hair. Rachel had no doubt who the girl was.

"You must be Brooke." Rachel took in the young woman who was Rye's and Max's baby sister. She looked like a willowy female version of them.

Rye kept an arm around his little sister's shoulders and reached out to grab Rachel's hand with the other. "This is Rachel Swift. Rachel, this is our sister, Brooke Harper."

"Rachel is Max's girlfriend." Stefan enunciated each word as he looked at Brooke.

Brooke glanced from Stefan to Rye and back again. "What do you mean Max's girlfriend? I thought you always took the cover role."

Rye seemed eager to avoid his sister's question. He turned to the doctor. "How long do you think it will be before we can see him?"

"Oh, a couple of hours," the doctor informed them. He told the group to wait, and they would be called in one at a time to see him.

Rachel felt Brooke's eyes on her as they settled in to wait.

* * * *

Rachel felt very alone and awkward any time Rye got up to go somewhere. After the doctor came out to announce that Max had come through his surgery, Rye decided his appetite had come back. Neither one of them had eaten breakfast that morning, but Rachel still couldn't stand the thought of food. Rye ambled off toward the cafeteria with Callie in tow. Rachel immediately wished she had gone with him. All during the long morning, Rye had been the one supporting her. He'd held her close while she cried and wrapped his arm around her shoulder as they waited. She'd found herself holding on to his hand even after Max had been declared in the clear.

It was easy to depend on Rye Harper. He wasn't in his uniform, so she was forced to see past the trappings of his office. Rye wasn't anything like Tommy. He didn't use his position to get things or intimidate people. He served the people around him, and they loved him for it. She could even forgive him for running a trace on her. If she had the resources, she would probably do the same for someone she cared about.

"So, you're dating Max." Brooke Harper sat on the sofa across from her, looking directly at Rachel. Now that her brother was all right, she was calm and collected.

The nineteen-year-old beauty tapped her foot impatiently against the carpet. She was dressed in jeans and a chic silk shirt. Though Rachel was thirty, she found herself strangely intimidated. Stefan Talbot was doing nothing to help her out. He sat beside Brooke. The look on his aristocratic face told Rachel he was concerned.

"I don't know if we're dating." Rachel forced herself to look Brooke and Stefan in the eyes. She might be intimidated, but she wasn't about to let them know. "I suppose it's casual." It wasn't. Her heart was fully engaged, but they didn't need to know that, either. It seemed to Rachel like she was about to get the "leave my brothers alone" lecture.

Brooke's laugh was anything but humorous. "Bullshit. If it was a casual relationship, then Rye would be the cover. That's the way they work in the outside world."

Rachel knew she probably looked confused. Stefan leaned forward in his seat. His hazel eyes were serious as he explained some things to her. "When Max and Rye are at home in Bliss, they're completely open about their relationships with women. It's different in the outside world. When they leave the county, Rye tends to pose as the current female's boyfriend, and Max is the supportive brother."

Brooke's arms came across her chest. "Rye is always the boyfriend. Max is always the one in the closet. He likes it that way. Max doesn't want the responsibility." She turned a saucy stare to her older companion. "A little like some other people I know, or has Jen finally gotten you to top her?" The last was said to Stefan with the long grin of a baby sister who knew way too much about the older men in her life.

"None of your business, Brooke," Stefan said in a tone that allowed no disobedience.

Brooke seemed completely unfazed by his authoritative tone, but then, Rachel couldn't blame her. She wasn't about to let the artist tell her what to do, either. Stefan Talbot oozed authority and not in the huggy way Rye did. Rachel could tell he was a man who would be in charge of everything in his life.

"As it happens," Stefan continued as though Brooke hadn't mentioned his personal life at all, "Max has turned around on the whole idea of responsibility. You know they stopped sharing about a year ago?"

The last bit was spoken to Brooke, but Rachel found herself leaning in. She wanted to know what had happened.

Brooke nodded. Her glossy golden brown hair shook. "Max was brooding. He always does that. Then Rye finds a girl, and Max comes back."

"Well, Max found a girl this time, and he's not sharing," Stefan said with a shrug.

Brooke's mouth dropped open. "You've got to be kidding me. Did you see the way Rye looked at her? He couldn't keep his hands off her. And Max won't share?" Cold blue eyes turned to Rachel. "Or is it someone else? What's wrong, city girl? Are we country folk too sexually liberated for you?"

There was something about her mocking tone that just set Rachel on edge. Deep inside, Rachel knew that one of the reasons she'd survived on the run for so long was the complete suppression of her personality. She'd become an automaton on the run. She'd become sweet and passive. She'd tried to be completely unthreatening. It was a reaction, she supposed. Tommy had always said that her forceful personality was the very thing that made him want to break her to his will. It hadn't been hard to act sweet. She was sweet, for the most part. But now Brooke Harper was pushing all the buttons that brought out her alpha self. Rachel took a firm hold on her inner bitch and tried to be patient.

"Max is the only one who asked me out." Rachel could feel her face flushing.

"Max believes you could never handle a ménage relationship," Stefan said. To Rachel's ears, it was said with an air of superiority.

"She's obviously just some pretty girl who wants to play around with Max." Brooke turned to Stefan, dismissing her entirely. "She isn't even smart enough to go for Rye. Rye would buy her stuff and treat her like a princess. She's the idiot who goes after Max." Brooke glanced back at Rachel. "Let me tell you, sister, the first time you piss Max off, you'll go running back home to your uptight mama."

And just like that, her inner bitch won. Rachel watched as Brooke actually leaned back a little. "First of all, I am not your sister, and if I was, I would put you on your ass right now. You are a rude little girl who has no right to talk to people the way you just spoke to me. You don't even know me, but you're judging me, aren't you? Your brothers would be ashamed of the way you just spoke to me. I haven't done anything except spend time with Max. I care about your brother, and I care about Rye, too. He's a good man who doesn't need his bratty little sister running around behind his back causing him grief."

Brooke opened her mouth to speak, but Stefan quickly covered it with his hand. "No, sweetheart, she's summed you up nicely. Please continue with your tirade, Ms. Swift. I am utterly fascinated. She called you sexually stifled. Please address this accusation."

"Screw you, Talbot," Rachel said heatedly. He seemed amused, and she didn't like being an object of entertainment for him. "I am just as sexually liberated as the next woman. I don't care that Max and Rye like to share. I wish to hell they would. That shower scene this morning would have ended more pleasantly."

Rachel felt her face go red. She shouldn't have mentioned that.

"Shower scene?" Brooke's prior distaste had been replaced with an almost expectant look of curiosity.

Stefan smiled like the Cheshire Cat. "Did you hop in with the wrong brother, sweetheart? How close did Rye get to the promised land before his conscience took over?"

Rachel sighed and sat back down. Her anger deflated as she thought about how lonely Rye had looked this morning. "It was a mistake. We quickly corrected it. Max and I are together. I'm going to honor what he wants." *Even if it kills me.*

Brooke sat forward and looked Rachel directly in the eyes. "I know my brothers. They won't be truly happy unless they're in a ménage. They need each other in ways the rest of us can't understand. Our parents were gone by the time I was seven. Rye and Max raised me. They're halves of a whole. They can try to find a woman and live on their own, but I think they'll be miserable. Do you want them to be miserable? If you can't handle it, then I think you should leave."

Rachel leaned in and didn't flinch. She had been planning to leave. She knew she was in far too deep with the brothers after this morning. Seeing Max lying on the ground had nearly torn out her heart. Before she had thought she couldn't afford to fall in love with one man, much less two. Now she realized there was no way she could walk away. She'd fallen into their trap and couldn't get out. There was no choice. She would have to work to make it all right. "I'm not going anywhere, Brooke. Get used to it. Did this little talk work on their other girlfriends?"

Brooke shrugged. "Usually."

Stefan shook his index finger at her. "One of these days, Brooke, you are going to find yourself a man who can handle you. I live for that day."

Brooke smiled smugly. "I'm sure you do. You'll grow old waiting for it to happen. Besides, if my little talk with Rachel here doesn't work, then I'm sure once she gets a load of Max's temper, she'll head out, and my brothers can find someone suitable. I'm already looking. I have a few prospects at my school I think they'll like."

Rachel stood back up and leaned over the younger woman. If she was staying, then it was time to stake her claim. "You bring those women around my men, honey, and don't expect them to come back in one piece. As for Max's temper, I've had a full dose of it. Guess what? I wasn't impressed. Our little fight ended with him apologizing nicely and playing my slave for the evening. I can handle Max, and I can certainly handle Rye. If you want to stay on my good side, I suggest you keep your friends away from my men. If you don't…well, I'm ready for a fight if you are."

Brooke looked at Stefan. "Is she serious? Did she really fight with Max and win?"

"She put Max on his ass in front of most of the population of Bliss," Stefan replied with a silky smile. "The truth of the matter is I wholeheartedly approve of her. She's perfect for them. She just has to make them see that she can handle what they need."

"Is there a video? Because I would really like to see Max beg." A brilliant smile crossed Brooke's face. It made her look younger. She popped up from her seat and suddenly looked like the young girl she was. "I'm so excited." She threw her arms around Rachel. "I'll start designing your dress immediately. It's going to be perfect."

"My dress?" Rachel was a little stunned at how fast Brooke had changed from overly protective sister to welcoming potential sister-in-law.

Brooke gestured up and down her body, indicating her very chic clothes. "I'm a designer. Mostly sportswear and lingerie, but I have an amazing wedding dress in mind for you. Sorry about the whole bad-girl routine. You have no idea how many women just use my brothers for sex."

"It's been terrible for them," Stefan interjected wryly.

"Now that I know you're the one," Brooke said, ignoring the artist, "I can be excited."

It was time to slow things down. Brooke wasn't the one who had to confront the problems with this scenario. "Look, I'm crazy about Max, and I really think I could love Rye, too, but they've been adamant about wanting a regular, ordinary relationship. I just can't tell them I'm keeping them both and set a date."

Brooke looked slightly perplexed. "Why not? That's the way life is. You say what you want, and then you go get it."

Stefan sighed and shook his head. "She's exceptionally young and sheltered. Rachel is right. If she tells them she wants the ménage all of a sudden, they will both be suspicious. She needs to get them to see that it can work."

"How do I do that?" Rachel was really interested in the answer to that question.

Stefan sat back, his hands steepling in front of his chest. He was such a decadent-looking thing. "I think I have a plan."

\* \* \* \*

Tommy Lane watched as his woman clung to another man. He stood in the shadows because it wasn't time yet to let his presence be known. Liz looked bad. He didn't like the way she'd changed her hair. When he had her back, he would force her to return to her natural color. The reddish blonde made her look like a whore.

Of course, the asshole she'd been holding hands with earlier made her look like a whore, too. Tommy felt his gut churn as he watched the tall man with brown hair return from the cafeteria. He took a seat beside Liz, and she immediately wound her fingers through his. The man looked surprised at first, but then settled beside her. His pleasure in the touch was obvious. When she'd rested her head on his shoulder, Tommy could feel the other man's satisfaction as though it was an actual physical thing.

He hated the way the other people in the party smiled and whispered. They obviously liked the fact that Liz was cuddling against the man for comfort. They approved. They couldn't possibly know she already belonged to someone else. She had lied again.

When, Tommy wondered, was she going to learn?

She belonged to him. He'd known it the moment they met. She'd looked at him with her big green eyes, and she'd wanted him. She'd played hard to get. She was that type. She was a tease. She'd gone out with him, let him spend money on her, and then when it was time to pay up, she'd pushed him away.

Tommy remembered it like it was yesterday.

\* \* \* \*

"Thank you for the evening," Liz said politely. She stood at the door to her little townhouse.

She was trying to play it cool, but Tommy had seen the way she looked at him. She wanted him. "You're welcome. It doesn't have to end, you know."

"I'm afraid I have to be up early for work," she said.

But her eyes were telling him yes. Tommy pulled her close. Her body was delicate against the rough hardness of his. She was a soft woman, and she needed a man to tell her what she wanted. She needed a man to keep her in line. She struggled, but that was just what women did. They liked to tease a man.

"I want you," Tommy said, making his intentions plain. He was a straightforward guy. "You belong to me." He covered her mouth with his. She tried to keep her mouth closed, but he was stronger. She tried to pull away. She didn't realize that just made him hotter. Or maybe she did. He loved how hard she fought and how easy it was for him to hold her. He couldn't wait to get between her legs. She would know she was his once he'd fucked her.

Liz cried out, the sound sweet to his ears. He shoved her against the wall and rubbed his hard cock against her, letting her know she had some work to do. It was a woman's job to satisfy a man, and he intended to make sure she did her job.

"Are you okay, Liz?"

Tommy's head came up. He saw that two of her neighbors were standing on the sidewalk looking up at them. It was a couple walking their dog. The neighbor was a big man, but the large dog at his side was what concerned Tommy. Liz was able to push away from him.

"Hello, Claire, I was hoping to talk to you," Liz said suddenly in a shaky voice.

The woman practically ran up the walk. The man stood and watched.

"Let's go inside and talk," Claire said, holding Liz's hand. "You can show me that website you told me about."

"Good night, Thomas," Liz said. Tommy could hear her voice trembling with passion.

\* \* \* \*

He'd been forced to make a strategic retreat that first night, but he'd thought about her all night. He'd gone home and masturbated just thinking about her soft body.

Then the bitch had stopped taking his calls.

It was just like a woman. She'd used him and then moved on. Someone should have warned her that no one moved on from Tommy Lane. Unfortunately, the ones who had tried in the past couldn't talk anymore.

Liz Courtney had proven to be a stubborn bitch. She'd sent back his gifts, so he'd shown her. He had left that little yipping thing she called a dog on her doorstep one night with its throat slit. That was when she'd gotten a restraining order. It had effectively put his career on hold. His partner, Eric Weldon, had tried to talk him out of pursuing the luscious Ms. Courtney further, but he'd understood when Tommy told him that he needed closure. Besides, Eric was dirty as the day was long. Tommy had a load of shit on him. He wouldn't get trouble from his partner. Eric had been the one to alert him that someone in this piss ant town was looking for her. He would get his closure.

She was holding the hand of one brother while the one Tommy had almost managed to kill lay in a hospital bed. He'd decided to kill the cowboy when he'd seen him kiss Rachel. She was staying at his house. God, she was such a whore.

He was going to kill her, and then she wouldn't have this hold on him anymore. He could move on once she was dead.

Of course, he thought with a smile, he'd fuck her first. She'd know what kind of a man he was then.

Tommy sank back into the shadows. His first attempt at taking out her lover had failed, but he'd try again. Now it looked like he'd have to kill both brothers, and then little Liz would be all his.

# Chapter Nine

Rye could feel his hands trembling as Rachel leaned back, and Max spread her legs. Her head fell backward. All that lovely hair was spread out on the bed like a strawberry blonde waterfall. Max was on his belly with his face between her thighs. He breathed in the scent of her soaking wet pussy and then swiped at it with his tongue.

"Oh, God, Max," Rachel sighed. Her lips parted as Max settled in. She looked down her body to stare at Max with those big green eyes.

Rye watched silently as his brother licked Rachel from her little rosebud all the way to her throbbing clit. From his vantage point, he could see that her clit was an engorged jewel just waiting to explode. It was so beautiful to Rye. Her pussy was bare and soft. It was perfectly plump and juicy.

"You taste so fucking good." Max groaned and proceeded to show her how much he liked her taste. His tongue swirled all around her pussy. He parted the labia with his fingers. He licked long strokes into her cunt. Even from where he was standing, Rye could tell his brother's face was getting coated in her juices.

Rachel was in ecstasy. He loved the sounds she made as she moved toward orgasm. Her lovely chest was heaving. Rye could see her pink-and-brown nipples were tight and ready for some man to come along and suck them like the sweet berries they were. He wanted to be that man. He would lick her little nipples and pull them one after the other into his greedy mouth. He would suck them until she couldn't take it anymore. He would give her just the bare edge of his teeth. He knew just how much to bite down so the little pain bloomed into pleasure. Between his mouth on her breasts and Max's tongue fucking her pussy, Rachel wouldn't be able hold off her orgasm. It would overwhelm her. She would come all over Max's mouth, and then, oh, then it would be their turn. Then they would take their scrumptious lover and fill her up with their cocks.

She would be so small between them. He would press against her back and push her down onto Max's hard cock. Max would curse because he wanted to fuck, but he'd hold off and wait for Rye. Rye would gently work the lube into the little rosette of her ass. His fingers would go first. He would marvel at how tight she was going to be, and his cock would strain. By the time he pushed into that hot little hole, he would be ready to explode.

"Rye." His name sounded like a plea on her lips. "Ryan, come here."

There was no question of refusing her. He moved forward, his hand on his cock. He hadn't realized he'd been stroking himself while he watched his brother and Rachel. Max never even looked up from his place at Rachel's pussy. He just ate her pussy like there was nothing else in the whole world.

"Yes, Rachel baby?" Rye would give her anything she wanted. His voice was husky. His hand stroked up and down his engorged cock.

"I want to taste you."

He shuddered.

"Ryan, fuck my mouth."

He nodded because there was no way he would deny her. He straddled her chest. The cheeks of his ass caressed her perfect breasts. Her hands came up to cup his rear, and he hissed when she lightly dug in her nails.

"You're mine, Rye," she said with purpose. Her eyes were intense on him. "You're mine, and so is Max."

"Yes," Rye heard himself saying as he lined up his throbbing dick with her lush mouth. Her lips teased the tip. "We're yours. We belong to you, baby. We belong together."

She sucked him inside, and Rye knew he'd found heaven.

\* \* \* \*

Rye woke up with a start. He looked down at the sheets and cursed profusely.

"This is fucking insane," he bitched as he wiped his cum-covered hand across the sheet. He would have to wash it again. It was the third time this week he'd ruined the sheets on his bed. He'd had more wet dreams since Max had come home from the hospital than he'd had in all of his teen years.

Rye shook his head and headed for the little bathroom down the hall. There still wasn't any hot water, but he didn't need it. He needed a fuckload of cold water. He might never take another hot shower again. He changed out of his ruined boxers into a fresh pair. He'd done three loads of his own laundry this week. Rachel was going to think he was a laundry freak. He opened the door and started down the hall to the bathroom.

"Good morning." Rachel stood waiting for him in the hallway.

Just like that, his dick was back at full attention. She was in a tank top and a pair of Max's boxers. They were too big and rode low on her hips, leaving a strip of perfect skin exposed. She was soft and sexy in the morning. She looked liked she'd just rolled out of bed. It was all Rye could do to not cup himself and run away. He hoped she didn't notice his painful condition.

"I'm making breakfast for the three of us." She had a ridiculously bright smile on her face. She lit up his world. "It's pancakes and sausage. Max's favorite." She touched the middle of his chest. "Tomorrow, it's your turn. I promise to make French toast, bacon, and grits. How does that sound?"

He clenched his jaw and forced himself to be polite. He did not, in any way, give any indication of what he truly wanted to do. He wanted to drag her back to the bed, spread her legs, and relieve the ache in his groin. Then he would be satisfied with "his turn." "Yes, that sounds nice."

She bounced a little. He'd noticed that about her. She was always moving. She had more energy than anyone he knew. She couldn't stand still. She bounced, and the bouncing made her tits wiggle. Rye decided he was going to throw himself off the roof. It would be an easier death than the death by sexual frustration he was going to suffer from Rachel.

"Good." She sounded relieved. "I don't want to leave you out. Now, I have to go back to work today. Can you handle the beast?"

Rye snorted. "I've been handling him since we were born, Rachel. I think I'll manage."

"If he gives you any trouble, just tell me." Rachel put one hand on her hip, and Rye loved the sassy sound of her voice. "We've come to an arrangement, Max and I. He behaves, and I don't dump food on his head."

Rye laughed, genuinely amused at the antics of his brother's woman. The hospital had been more than happy to release Max as soon as he could physically handle leaving. He was a beast when he was sick. The nurses had been ready to sedate him a few minutes after he'd become conscious. Even Brooke had conceded that he probably deserved it. Only Rachel could placate him.

And she had taken care of him. She'd been the most patient nurse Max could have hoped for. She had followed the doctor's orders to the letter. She made sure Max took his prescriptions and stayed in bed for the first few days. Unfortunately, even the most patient of women have their breaking point. When Max complained about the soup she made, Rachel very calmly dumped it over his head and told him to go to hell. Rye smiled just remembering the incident. Rye had eaten the soup Rachel gave him, though it had been lacking salt, and declared the meal delicious. Max, after cleaning up, had eaten a bowl himself. He then politely thanked the chef. Rye knew Rachel was discovering the trick to handling Max. Max needed firm, nonnegotiable boundaries. Once they were set, Max knew how to behave. Max had been a perfect angel ever since.

Well, he was perfect around Rachel. He was crabby around his own brother. Rye knew why. Max wasn't used to being laid up. He was used to working hard every day for at least ten hours. Rachel was forcing him to stay off his feet, and it was killing Max. Today was the first day he was allowed to be back on a horse. Rye also suspected Max was having some of the same trouble Rye was experiencing. Rachel was worried that he was too fragile for sex. Of course, Rye thought ruefully, Max had hope of getting some. Rye was hopeless.

"I'll make sure he takes it easy." Rye didn't want her to worry about Max all day. His breath caught at the way her eyes gleamed in the early morning light. He would be able to handle the close contact with her if it was all just lust. The trouble was he was falling more and more in love with her every day.

She looked wistful. "I wish I could stay, but Stella really needs me. I've been off for almost a week, and Jen is getting really tired of pulling doubles. I think she's looking forward to just working the dinner shift. Stella promised she'd bring in another girl soon."

"Why do you have to go back to work at all?" He hated the thought of her being on her feet for ten hours. He loved that diner, but the women there worked damn hard. He'd seen how tired Rachel could be after a shift. "You have to know Max would support you, sweetheart."

He would, too. He just would be very quiet about it. He already intended to send Callie off to buy her some clothes. She barely had enough to make it through a week. Rye was planning on "finding" some old clothes Brooke had left behind and offering them to Rachel. He would have to remind himself to make sure he took the tags off first.

"I know. Trust me, I've heard the lecture. Would it surprise you to know that I like to have my own money? I don't mind working. I like the diner. It's fun to talk to everyone. I'm just not cut out to be a live-in girlfriend, Rye." She leaned forward. "I've been thinking about getting a place in town. Jen says she has an extra room, and Stefan told me his guesthouse is free."

Rye felt his body go rigid. He had a sudden and extreme need to beat the shit out of his closest friend. Rye knew what Stef kept in the guesthouse. Stef kept his playroom in the guesthouse. It was where he kept his submissives. If Stefan thought for one second he could take Rachel in and begin training her, he would have to think again.

"I'll have a conversation with Stefan about that," Rye heard himself say. It came out more threatening than he'd intended. He consciously softened his stance and his voice. "I think you should stay here, Rachel."

Her green eyes were guileless. "I will for as long as Max needs me. Then I think I should get my own place. I know this has been rough on you. The last thing you need is your brother's girl hanging around all the time."

"Rachel, I love having you here." He did. He just wished they were together.

She turned, and he caught sight of her perky little ass encased in cotton boxers. It made his mouth water. "I think you love having me cook," she said with a shrug. "See you at breakfast."

He watched her walk toward the kitchen and heard Max's low greeting.

"Morning, gorgeous," his brother said. Rye knew he was kissing her.

Rye walked into the bathroom thinking about just how much he liked having Rachel around. He turned on the shower. With Max injured, there had been no question of Rye staying with friends. Rye had taken some time off to take care of the stables while Max was down. Working with horses again was making him think about making a permanent change. He'd taken the job as sheriff because, at the time, they had needed a steady income. Brooke had still been in grade school, and money had been tight. Rye had known he was the one who could hold down a job without being murdered by his coworkers, so he'd taken one for the team. He'd started as a deputy. When the old sheriff had retired, Rye had easily been voted into office. No one else wanted the job. But his real love was working with horses, like Max did every day. The stables paid now. Harper Stables had an excellent reputation, and more work was coming in every day. If Rye quit, he could help Max and teach riding lessons. He wanted to work with his brother again.

He wanted to live here with Max and Rachel, too. The last week had proven that to him. Every evening they had dinner together. Max sat across from Rye, and Rachel sat happily in the middle. She was in the middle of everything. When they sat down to watch television, Rachel plopped down between them just like she belonged there. When they went out, she sat in the middle of the long bench seat of Max's vintage Ford truck. She insisted on the three of them doing things together. They'd watched movies, played games, and talked about everything under the sun. She'd made it easy for him to almost believe he was a part of this little family she and Max seemed to be forming.

*What if she could handle a ménage? What if she wants it?*

Rye stepped under the cool water and cursed. He was hard again, and the water wasn't helping. He wrapped his hand around his dick and started to brush his thumb over the head. He was going to go blind. He just knew he was.

\* \* \* \*

Max's hands slid down to cup his girlfriend's perfect cheeks. He pulled her close and didn't try to disguise the erection he was sporting. It had been days since he'd gotten inside her. It was starting to make him crazy.

"Hello, gorgeous," Max breathed as he leaned down to slant his mouth across hers.

Rachel softened against him and wrapped her arms around his neck. She didn't protest as his tongue swept in to play with hers. He hauled her up so her feet were dangling. It was the only way to get her little pussy where he wanted it. He rubbed himself against her. He knew it made him a caveman, but he wanted to mark her as his. He wanted her to get a tattoo on that perfect ass of hers that read Property of the Harper Brothers.

Max set her down. His brain just went there all the time now. He couldn't stop thinking about Rachel between him and Rye. "What's for breakfast?"

"Pancakes and sausage," Rachel replied with a suspicious gleam in her eyes.

Max kissed her forehead gently and went to sit down at the kitchen table. He was very careful since Rachel was looking at him. He didn't want her to figure out what he was thinking. He had more than one thing he needed to hide from her today. He schooled his features to express nothing but innocence.

"Oh, God, what are you thinking?" Rachel looked utterly horrified. "Who are you going to kill?"

"What?" Max asked, holding his hands up in confusion.

She rounded the table and leaned over. Max couldn't help but notice she wasn't wearing a bra. If he leaned in just a little bit, he could see the curve of her breasts and the faintest hint of nipple.

"Eyes up, mister," Rachel ordered in what he'd come to think of as her "drill sergeant" voice. His eyes obediently came up. He'd learned when it was in his best interests to obey her immediately. His baby was one tough cookie, and he was man enough to admit he needed her to be that way. He would walk all over her otherwise. That would make for one boring relationship. Rachel kept him on his toes.

"Sorry, baby." He would try to distract her with charm. He had some of that. He smiled and pulled her hand into his. He tugged her down onto his lap. "I can't help it. I get distracted by your breasts.

They're really pretty. And I'm really, really horny. We haven't had sex in days. It's killing me, Rach."

She rolled her eyes and sighed. Her arms went around his neck. "Max, you just had surgery. You haven't even had the stitches out yet. The doctor said we should wait a few days."

"It's been almost a week." He put a little whine in his voice. Maybe if she thought he was just horny, she would forget her suspicions. It was imperative that she not figure out what he had done after she'd gone to sleep. "I promise I could be very still. I would lie perfectly still, and you could do all the work."

She grinned. It did strange things to his heart. "That sounds so tempting. I'll call the doctor today, and I'll see if we can get him to let you off the leash." She kissed his cheek. She got up and went to the stove, where she poured out pancake batter. Max relaxed.

She rounded on him suddenly. "You're sure you're not planning something terrible?"

She knew him far too well. He grimaced inwardly. This was where Rye would come in handy. Rye could distract her. Rachel, Max had decided, was far too much woman for one man. He needed his brother because Max had figured out that a tag team approach was required when Rachel got saucy. But he was all on his own now. He didn't like the feeling.

"Baby, I'm just planning on doing a little light work around the barn. I'm going to spend some time with Sunflower, and then I'll have Rye drive me into Del Norte for my checkup. That's my plan." It was true. It was part of his plan. He didn't mention the stop he intended to make.

Her eyes narrowed, and he wondered briefly if she could make that spatula into a weapon. He thought she probably could. Max sighed. He could make it into one, too. He could pull her over his lap and shove those boxers off her hips, then spank that pert little rear. He wouldn't hurt her. He'd just get her bottom all pink and pretty. He'd rather use his hand, though, he decided.

"What did you just think?" Rachel asked breathlessly.

Rye stood in the doorway. He had on jeans and a T-shirt. His hair was still wet from his shower. "He was wondering how you would handle it if he pulled you across his lap and spanked you with your spatula. You should use your hand, Max. It would be better."

Rachel's mouth fell open. She looked between the two of them like she was trying to figure out what to say.

Max pointed at Rye. "He said it."

Rye shrugged. "He was thinking it."

"So were you."

Rye's face fell. Max saw him look down at the crotch of his jeans. "Damn it." He turned and walked back down the hall. Max knew exactly where he was going.

"What's wrong with him?" Rachel looked concerned as his brother marched off.

Max smiled broadly. Rye had done his job. She wasn't thinking about his potential plans anymore. She set a plate in front of him. "I guess he's not hungry," Max lied.

His brother was hungry, all right. He'd been hungry since the minute he laid eyes on Rachel. Max didn't blame him. He had been lucky to see her first, or Max knew he might be the one spending an awful lot of time in the bathroom. The thing was, Max thought as he began to dig into his breakfast, he was starting to believe this whole thing could work. There was a light at the end of the tunnel, and it was getting brighter every day. The last week had been a bit of a revelation. Rachel had been perfectly comfortable with Rye. She seemed to enjoy being with both of them.

That was the trick. Getting her comfortable being at the center of their ménage would change everything. Once she realized that they intended to worship the ground she walked on, the sex would be easy. She was beginning to see that no one in Bliss would look down on her for being involved with two men. Once Rachel realized she would be accepted, and that they loved her, she would understand that it was okay to love them both back. Max knew he and Rye could make it so good for her that she would wonder why she hadn't had two men before. She wouldn't want to go back.

A sense of contentment took root. He had a plan. He'd formulated it during the long hours he'd been forced to stay in bed. After he'd woken up in the hospital, he'd realized exactly what he wanted out of life. He wanted everything, and he wasn't willing to compromise. He wanted Rachel to marry him and Rye. He wanted her to have their children. He wanted happily ever after for all three of them. He would have to be ruthless and purposeful to get what he wanted. Part of his plan was figuring out just what Rachel was running from. In all the discussions the three of them had indulged in over the last week, Rachel had been silent on the subject.

Max munched thoughtfully on his sausage as he watched his woman swaying to some music she heard in her head while she flipped pancakes for Rye's breakfast.

Last night, while she'd slept peacefully in their big bed, he'd slipped away. He'd moved quietly through the house and out to her car. She'd been living in it. It only made sense that she kept her secrets there. After thoroughly going over every inch of the old Jeep, he'd found a seam in the floorboard. The items she kept in that little hidey-hole had just brought up more questions.

He'd found her pitiful stash of cash. She'd saved three hundred dollars from her tips, and there was a check she hadn't cashed yet for another three hundred and fifty dollars. It was the sum of her wealth. Max's heart seized at the thought of her having so little to her name.

Which wasn't Rachel Swift. Elizabeth Courtney or Shannon Matthews was her real name. He'd found identification with both of those names in an envelope. Max wasn't sure which one was actually her real name, but he intended to find out. He intended to discover just what had happened in her past to send her running. Then he would sit down with Rye and tell his brother what he wanted. He would tell Rye he wanted them to marry Rachel. Together they would take care of her problem. He just wanted to make sure it wasn't anything that would compromise his brother's position as an officer of the law. Once he was sure of that, he'd bring in Rye.

"Are you sure you didn't find out the name of the hunter who accidently shot you?" Rachel asked suspiciously.

He shook his head. "No, baby."

She didn't look convinced. Max took a quick swallow of coffee and tried to look normal. She put Rye's plate down. "Where did he go? I swear that man disappears four times a day. What is he doing in that room?"

Max choked on his laughter. He knew exactly what his brother was doing. "I have no idea."

"Rye, breakfast is ready," she shouted down the hall.

Max leaned back in his chair. He needed to get this plan going. His brother was going to go blind if he didn't stop masturbating.

# Chapter Ten

Stefan took the clothes Lana offered him. They were perfectly folded. Stefan inspected them and nodded shortly. It was her cue, and she did exactly what was expected of her. The lovely blonde sank to her knees gracefully and sat waiting. Her head was submissively down. Her hands were on her thighs facing upward. She could sit like that for hours. There was nothing quite like a well-trained sub, Stefan thought.

Stefan turned and walked to the small closet in the front hall of his guesthouse. He placed her clothes in the drawer he had designated as hers, and then shut the door. She wouldn't see her designer suit, La Perla lingerie, and Jimmy Choos again until late Sunday evening. Until then, she would either remain naked or wear exactly what he selected for her. There would be no deviation from his requirements. She would not complain or suggest something different. Lana was close to perfect.

So why was his head so filled with someone else?

He looked over his sub. She was his match in every way. Lana was well educated. She maintained her lovely body with daily trips to the gym. She was roughly thirty-five, but Stef knew she already had regular appointments with a plastic surgeon. She was stunning and had no intention of being anything else. Most importantly, she knew who she was and what she wanted. It was what he absolutely required from any woman he "dated."

Jennifer Waters was this woman's opposite. The little painter could only be described as a hot mess. She was barely twenty-two and had no idea who she was. Her work showed great promise, but she needed years to temper her undisciplined ways. She had come to Bliss in the hopes that she could learn from him, but Stefan didn't teach. Not art. He was renowned in the art world as an upcoming master, but he didn't have any idea how to teach what he did.

He also didn't know how to get a woman out of his head. She was far too young to be what he needed her to be. Lana was a much better choice. She was cultured and sophisticated. There was never a hair out of place or a nail chipped. Jen's nails always had paint under them. Stefan could tell what colors were on her palette by looking at her nails. He was utterly fascinated with her hands.

"Up," he said, eager to get his mind off troublesome subjects.

Lana rose with little effort. She stood calmly as he looked her over. She wasn't waiting for his judgment. Stef had no doubt that she knew exactly how good she looked and how much he wanted her sexually. Stefan knew she was merely waiting for his next command.

"Present yourself to me," he said quietly.

She walked to the middle of the austerely decorated room and leaned over the plush sofa. Her hands pressed against the arm. She placed her well-formed ass high in the air. Stefan sighed, satisfied with her obedience. He almost never needed to discipline Lana. Occasionally, she was late due to her job. That resulted in time spent over his lap or in the whipping chair, depending upon the degree of the infraction, but that was a rare occurrence. Lana didn't play at this like so many others. She didn't purposefully disobey to force him to discipline her. It was why she continued to be invited to his playroom. Stefan ran his hand down her straight spine and let his fingers drift to the cleft in her ass. He loved the sleek lines of her body. Her legs went on for days. She really was a work of art. He felt his interest rising just as he heard the car pulling up the drive.

Stefan looked out the bay window and saw the beige-and-white SUV pulling up. The driver slammed on the brakes and then proceeded to jam his door shut. Stef smiled. It was Rye. He had expected that Max would be the one to violently assault him, but he was happy to see Rye. It proved that Rachel was a smooth co-conspirator. He'd left the choice of which brother to tell of his offer to her, and she'd chosen correctly. Rye was the one she needed to break. Max would follow along.

"We have company," Stef said, shoving his finger into her tight pussy anyway. She had been a very good girl. There was no reason to punish her because Rye was insanely jealous. It wouldn't be the first time Rye had walked in on him having sex.

Stef smiled, thinking about their shared youth. Max and Rye hadn't always just shared with each other. They'd enjoyed some of Stef's games, too. Stef remembered a particularly hot night when the three of them had shared a woman. His thumb reached up to swirl around Lana's clitoris. She moaned a bit. "Silent," Stef said, reminding her. "I'll let you know when you can make noise, darling."

She closed her lips and made no move to cover herself even when there was a knock on the door.

"Come in." Stefan added a second finger and picked up the pace. "Hold off until I give you leave."

Rye stalked through the door. "What the hell do you think you're doing, Stef?"

"Well, right now, I'm playing." He felt the heat of her pussy. She was ripe and wet. Lana was extremely responsive. Her body had been trained to receive pleasure, so she expected it. Stefan could feel the willpower it took for her to stand and allow him to pleasure her. It took discipline to do it. He admired discipline.

"Could you stop playing and talk to me for a minute?" Rye's question came out in an irritated hiss.

It didn't concern Stefan. He had an obligation. "No, you'll have to talk to me like this or wait until I've seen to my submissive." Stefan pressed his fingers into her clenching cunt and rotated. He knew exactly which spot to hit.

"Fuck this, Stef," Rye growled. "I have a serious problem with you."

He wasn't going to wait patiently. "Our guest is going to prove irritating, dear," Stefan said to his sub. "Perhaps you should come, and then we can pay him proper attention. Consider yourself off the leash."

Lana pushed back against his hand, fucking his fingers. She moaned loudly as he hit the perfect spot, and she went flying. A pretty blush covered her skin. She let her head fall forward and groaned as she extracted maximum satisfaction from her orgasm. When Stefan was sure she was done, he removed his fingers from her body, then turned to Rye.

"How may I help you today, Rye?" Stefan knew exactly what Rye took exception to, but he found himself anticipating the coming confrontation. He pulled a handkerchief out of his slacks pocket and gracefully wiped his hand. Lana silently sank to her knees, assuming the proper submissive position at his side. He let his hand find her hair to acknowledge her good behavior.

Rye did not look impressed. Stefan knew that most men wouldn't be able to take their eyes off the lovely sub, but Rye was different. "What the fuck do you mean by offering to take Rachel in?"

"Such language." Stefan laughed as he walked to the bar. He poured himself a couple of fingers of Scotch. It was ridiculously expensive, but he always had the best. "I merely offered the lovely Rachel a place to stay. I was being neighborly. She mentioned she was going to need a new home soon."

"She doesn't need anything from you." Rye paced the room, seemingly unable to stand still.

Stefan looked his best friend over. They had grown up together. Stefan's father was an eccentric millionaire who took a liking to Bliss and moved his son there. Stefan had stayed on with an army of servants even after his father had returned to his jet-setting lifestyle and the family mansion in Dallas. Rye and Max had been a big reason he chose to stay in the town. They were the brothers he'd never had.

Callie was as close as a sister. They, and everyone else in the offbeat town, were his family.

He wondered if Rye had any idea how much he looked like an angry bull at the moment. His normally happy-go-lucky friend was like a predatory animal circling an opponent. Stefan was suddenly very happy Rachel had made the right choice. Rye was the reasonable one. If she'd told Max, Stefan knew he would probably already be on his ass. Max wouldn't have asked questions. He would have done exactly what he had done since they were children. He would fight first and ask questions never. Max was pure pit bull.

"She apparently needs a place to stay," Stefan remarked negligently. "Luckily, I have this place. I think she'll find it very comfortable."

Rye's jaw looked like it was made of granite. Stefan knew his friend was holding on tightly to his rage. "Are you planning on training her?" He indicated the woman at Stef's side. "You getting rid of that one so you can move Rachel in? Do you really think Rachel is so weak-willed that she'll be your little slave?"

Now Stefan felt his own anger building. "First of all, there is nothing weak-willed about Lana. She is my guest, and I would prefer you treat her with respect." He looked down at his part-time submissive. "You have my permission to speak, sweetheart. Tell our intensely rude guest who you are and what you do for a living."

Lana's head came up. Stef could see Rye flush with embarrassment. He knew Rye hadn't meant to be rude, but the mistake would be corrected nonetheless.

"My name is Lana O'Malley. I'm the owner and CEO of True Line International. I'm worth roughly a billion dollars, depending on how the market goes. I enjoy my time with the master. It's how I relax. I make no apologies for my sexual desires, whoever you are. If you have a problem with it, I really don't care."

"I am sorry," Rye said sincerely. "I don't judge. As perverse as I've been on occasion, I really shouldn't. I'm just pissed off that your master here seems to think he can swoop in and take my girl."

Stefan raised a single eyebrow. "Your girl?"

"Max's girl." Rye corrected himself, sounding sheepish. He suddenly seemed fascinated with his boots.

"Then I have to ask, why Maxwell isn't here defending the lady?" Stefan walked to his friend and put an arm around his shoulder. "You really need to figure this out. I can see it's killing you. Why are the two of you denying your natures? We promised each other a long time ago that we wouldn't pretend." Stef remembered the day well. Callie had been there, too, and the four of them had sworn to be true to themselves no matter what.

"Max loves her." Rye's hoarse voice matched the weary look in his eyes. "She loves him. I can't screw it up for him."

"You love her, too. You have to know Max wouldn't want you left out."

Rye shook his head stubbornly. "I don't think Rachel would want that. She's a normal girl."

Stef sighed. "There's no such thing. If someone looks 'normal,' they're either hiding their kinks well or utterly denying who they are. I don't think Rachel is into denial. Have you asked her? Have you been honest about what the two of you need?"

Rye ran a frustrated hand through his hair, and every muscle in his body seemed bunched and tense. "Just stay out of it, Stef. It's none of your business. If I see you trying to tempt Rachel away from Max, I'll take care of it, and you won't like how I do it. Do you understand?"

Stefan put up his hands. He had no intention of staying out of it, but he wasn't going to argue with Rye. It was time to bring it down a notch. "Absolutely. Will I see you at the picnic tomorrow?"

Tomorrow was the Founder's Day gathering. It was the biggest event Bliss held. Stefan had plans for the brothers. He and Rachel had been plotting for almost a week.

"Yes." Rye seemed to make a conscious effort to calm down. Stefan knew that Rye usually attended, but Max stayed away from crowds. They tended to annoy him. "Rachel says we have to go. All of us. She's helping Stella out at her booth, but she's made it plain we're to put in an appearance. She wants Max to clean up his image or some nonsense."

Stef doubted there would be any image building for Maxwell beyond the fit he would throw when he realized what was happening. "I'll see you then."

Rye walked out, but Stefan was satisfied that he looked more contemplative than when he had walked in. His friend would think about what they had talked about all day. Rye would be ripe for the plucking when tomorrow came around. Stefan looked down at Lana.

"What do you think, dear?" She was a highly intelligent woman whose opinion he valued.

Lana's stared at the door that Rye had walked out of. "He's in love with her. She's an idiot if she doesn't want them. His brother is a twin, right? I have friends who will take them, if she's too much of a prude."

Stefan sat down and tapped his thighs. Lana immediately placed herself in his lap. "She isn't. She's very much looking forward to tomorrow. We'll need to stay in the main house. I'm giving them this place for the evening."

"He seemed adamant," Lana stated thoughtfully.

Stefan reached over and pushed a small button on the side table. A door slid open where there had appeared to be none. Lana showed no discomfort as two men walked out from the hiding space.

"I intend to give him a reason to stake his claim," Stef explained.

"I take it that was our mark?" asked Bay, the older of the brothers. Shane was silent, watching Lana with lust in his eyes.

"One of them," Stef replied. "Lana, dear, do you think they'll do?"

Stef watched as Lana looked over the two men thoughtfully. They were in their early twenties, and both had a rugged attractiveness to them. Stef had met the older of the two brothers when he bought a sculpture the man had done. It was a haunting piece of work, and Stef had sought out the artist. He'd been surprised to discover he was a rodeo cowboy. Stefan had struck up a strange friendship with the brothers. Now he would use them to his own ends. They would get something out of it, too, of course. Stefan Talbot was a great believer in reciprocity.

"Yes, I believe they will work quite nicely." She pouted a little as she looked back at him. "Are they only here to make the twins jealous, or did you have something else in mind, master?"

She knew him well.

"Shane, Bay." Stefan indicated that they could come closer. "My little slave would love for you to play with her." Stefan liked to watch. The brothers were out of their clothes before he could get another word out, but Lana waited patiently.

"Go on, dear," he said affectionately. "I believe they're ready. Ah, youth."

Lana fell to her knees and put that talented mouth around Bay's cock. Shane positioned himself to taste her pussy. Stefan sat back and enjoyed the show.

* * * *

Max stared at the computer in front of him.

Callie stood in the doorway, peering into his brother's office. Max could tell she was beginning to suspect he was using the computer for something he shouldn't. "Are you sure you don't need something, Max?"

Oh, he needed something. He needed better weaponry and a security system for the house and some bodyguards so he knew Rachel was never alone. Liz, he corrected. Her real name was Liz.

"Do you know where Rye is?" was all he asked.

Callie shook her head. "He's not supposed to be back in until Monday. Logan's staking out that T-intersection where no one ever stops." She shrugged apologetically. "We could use a new fridge in the break room, and the microwave is on the fritz."

"I tried his cell, and he didn't answer." Max just stared dumbly at the computer screen. He should have done the search at home, but he knew Rye had access to things he didn't. He'd gotten past Callie by saying he just needed to use the Internet to look up some directions. He guessed Rye's password on the second try and quickly found what he needed now that he had her real name.

Of course, if he had known what he would find, he would have brought Rye in from the beginning. He'd just been cautious. If Rachel was running from people she owed money to or was running from the cops, he would have handled the situation without Rye.

She was running from a cop, all right, but there was nothing about the situation that could compromise Rye's job. This was Rye's job. He was honor-bound to protect and serve, and Rachel needed both.

"He's in the Bronco, right?" Callie twirled her dark brown hair around her fingers thoughtfully. It was a habit she'd had since they were kids.

Max nodded. Rye had taken his county-issued vehicle when he left on his mysterious errand.

Callie sighed, and Max could tell she'd decided to shelve her curiosity. "I'll try raising him on the radio, then. Sometimes he forgets to charge his cell. Half the time that thing doesn't work, anyway. The coverage out here is iffy at best."

She walked off, and Max felt bad. He'd always been the one to see to things like that. He was more organized than Rye. Even when they were kids, Max had been the one to make sure Rye had everything he needed when it came to school. If it had been up to Rye, he would have never brought a lunch or had a pencil with him. Rye forgot, so Max took over. Max just handled that stuff for Rye when he was doing it for himself. He plugged in Rye's cell every night just before he plugged in his own. Last night, he'd put his on the charger and then charged the one he had bought for Rachel. It seemed an imposition to barge into Rye's room and force him to charge his phone.

When had that happened? When had he started worrying about his brother's privacy? Max didn't like it. Something was going to have to give, and soon. He needed to talk to Rachel. First, though, he needed to deal with the problem at hand.

Someone out there wanted to kill their woman.

Max didn't correct himself mentally this time. She was theirs. She just didn't know it yet. She was living with them, and they would wear her down. One day in the not too distant future, she would wake up between them and realize that they could make it work.

After he'd killed one Tommy Lane.

Max swore out loud as he looked over the newspaper articles. Tommy Lane had stalked the young insurance adjuster, and when he couldn't scare her into complying, he'd set her house on fire. Liz Courtney had barely gotten out with her life. He'd killed her dog and ruined her reputation at work. He'd made her life a living hell. The Dallas papers wondered where he had stuffed her body. None of it could be proven. Like so many other women, Liz had been caught in a legal Catch-22.

She'd disappeared a few mornings after the fire. Some witnesses said they saw her driving off in a sedan, but no one had seen her since then. There was some question as to whether the former officer had killed the woman and dumped her body. The prosecutors were in a bad position. They had no body and no witnesses. They couldn't prove the arson. Tommy Lane was a free man.

Max studied the picture of the man who had made Rachel's life a living hell. He was a rough-looking son of bitch. He was probably forty, and it looked like he'd gotten there the hard way. He was dressed in a crisp uniform, but there was something shady about him that no dress uniform could ever cover up.

Max glanced at the clock. It wasn't quite eight. Rachel wouldn't be getting off work for another hour and a half. He had time. He intended to be there when she left. He would follow her home. From now on, he would take her to and from work until he could convince her she didn't need to work at all. She was fairly safe at the diner. Both Stella and Hal carried guns, and they wouldn't hesitate to use them. Rye would make sure everyone in town knew what the fucker looked like and to shoot him on sight. They could make up a daring tale of self-defense later. Everyone in Bliss would back them up on it. They stuck together in Bliss, and Rachel was one of their own now.

Rye walked in. He placed his Stetson on a large filing cabinet and looked pointedly at his desk. "I was on my way home when Callie called. What are you doing here? And why the hell are you on my system? Do you know I can arrest you for that?"

"Arrest me later." Max turned the laptop around. "I know why Rachel ran."

Max got up and allowed his brother to sit. It didn't take long before Max saw Rye flush with rage. He knew exactly what his brother was feeling. He was feeling the extreme need to defend their woman.

"He's going to come after her," Max said quietly. "He won't be satisfied. He knows she's not dead, and I have no doubt he's looking."

Rye sat back. He ran a hand through his hair and shook his head as though trying to rid himself of some terrible image. "You're right. He's obsessed with her. He won't stop." Rye looked up at him. "You don't think...?" His eyes went to the spot on Max's arm where he'd had the stitches taken out earlier today.

Max wasn't sure. He went with logic. "I don't think so. Why would he have been quiet for a whole week? He's had numerous opportunities to take another shot at any one of us."

Rye stared at his chest. He was thinking about how close he'd come to losing his brother. Max knew because once he'd felt the same way. Rye had been in a car accident, and it had been the worst time of Max's life. He knew just how Rye felt, but he wanted to get back to the problem at hand, saving Rachel.

"How would he have found her?" Max asked.

Rye sighed. His face tightened, and there was guilt in his eyes when he looked at Max. "I put a call in to a couple of the PDs in Texas, mostly Houston and a couple of suburbs around there. I was just putting out some feelers. No one knew anything. She changed her hair color, and she lost a lot of weight."

The Rachel Swift who had come to Bliss bore little resemblance to the woman in the newspaper photos, though now, with proper and consistent meals, she was beginning to look more like herself. Max had been stuffing her, trying to get her to lose that gaunt, haunted look.

Rye continued. "But if this guy is as devious as he sounds, he would have known she had to have help. If I was him, I would have checked out her family."

"She doesn't have one." The papers had verified her stories. Rachel was alone on the world.

"Then I would check out the local women's shelters or maybe someone at the hospital. Someone helped Rachel. If he got to that person, he would know her fake identities. All he has to do is have a cop buddy call someone in one of those towns and make up a reason to be on the lookout for her. I tripped his little fail-safe when I put the trace on her. Damn, Max, if I had any idea this could happen, I never would have checked her out."

"It isn't your fault. We don't know that he's found her again. How are we going to protect her? I'm worried that she'll run if she thinks he's on her trail."

Rye was quiet for a moment as he thought. "Maybe you should run with her."

"No." Max had already thought of and discarded that possibility. "That isn't a life, Rye. Look what it did to her. She ran because she was all alone in the world. She isn't anymore. This is her home. Every person in this town will defend her. I won't let this asshole run our wife off, and I won't let him hurt her again."

A slow smile crossed Rye's face. His brother hadn't missed his intentional use of words. She wasn't their wife yet, but in Max's mind, it was only a matter of time.

"You said 'our,' Max."

For the first time in weeks, Max felt the gulf between them begin to shrink. He realized now that Rye needed him to say the words. Rye needed to know that he was willing to share Rachel. "I meant it. She's the one, and you know it."

Rye's smile turned slightly sad, but Max could feel something inside his brother relax. A tension that had been there since Rachel had come to town now loosened. Max was glad to see it go.

"I know," Rye said. "We've been waiting for her all of our lives, but we have to get her to recognize it."

Max nodded. "We will. First, we deal with this asshole."

"It won't be easy. We'll have to keep an eye on her."

"I think the whole town should keep an eye on her."

Rye looked thoughtful for a moment. "That is a fantastic idea. I have another one. We can get a PI working back in Dallas to come up with the dirt on this asshole. He needs to be in jail. I won't feel safe until he's behind bars. On Monday, we'll talk to the prosecutors. If we go back to Dallas with Rachel, it will make their job a lot easier. If Rachel testifies, maybe we can get him in jail without bond. He's made it plain he means to kill her."

"Let's get through the weekend first. Rach is so excited about the Founder's Day thing tomorrow. I can't bring myself to shake up her whole world. She's safe for now. We have no evidence that he knows where she is. We won't let her out of our sight. Sunday night, we'll explain everything to her. Hopefully, we'll both still be standing at the end." Max had no doubt that Rachel would be furious they had checked up on her. She would fight them, but this was one fight he meant to win.

"It's too important to ignore," Rye said solemnly. "We can't just hope she's going to tell us someday. We have to do what we can to get this guy in prison so he can't come after our woman again."

Max sighed as Rye started to make some calls. He didn't mention to his law-abiding brother that he had no intention of Lane seeing the inside of a jail cell. They were too easy to break out of. There was parole and prison overcrowding to consider. No, there wouldn't be any cushy prison cells for Tommy Lane. There was only one way Max would be able to sleep at night.

He was going to kill him.

# Chapter Eleven

Rachel stood behind the counter of the diner and looked at her boss. "You're sure you don't need me to stay the whole shift?"

She was hoping beyond hope that the answer was no. She was anxious to get back home and check up on Max and Rye. Her heart did a little flip-flop at the word "home." She was starting to think of Harper Stables as her home. She loved the big house and the easy way the three of them shared it. After tomorrow night, they would share everything, she promised herself. She intended to make it impossible for them to deny her or themselves any longer.

Stella looked distracted. She was in full preparation mode for the big picnic and auction tomorrow. Rachel heard the doors to the diner open. "Don't worry about it. We've been slow all day."

Rachel took off her apron and walked around the counter to get her purse. She was stopped in her tracks by two cowboys. She took in the sight of the two men walking into the place like they owned it. Jen stopped beside her. Her hands were still holding the order she was taking out.

"Damn," Jen said under her breath. Her eyes widened as she watched the cowboys striding in.

Damn was right, Rachel thought, hiding her smile. Stefan had been correct about the Kent brothers. They were just about perfect for her purposes. They each had dark hair peeking out from their Stetsons. Their long legs looked strong in tight jeans and worn boots. They weren't twins, but there was no question they were brothers. Rachel was taken by their startlingly deep green eyes. They were young men, but there was no doubt that they were men.

"Ma'am," the taller one said, tipping his hat as he took a seat at the counter. His brother followed. Neither of them hid the fact that they were assessing the women in the room. Rachel rolled her eyes as the one on the right boldly stared at her chest.

"Who are they?" Jen leaned toward Rachel and kept her voice low.

"Friends of Stefan's." Rachel offered no other explanation. They really were friends of Stefan's. They were also about to be the bane of Max's and Rye's existence. She had to carefully school her face because she wanted to laugh. The Kent brothers probably acted a whole lot like the Harper twins had when they were arrogant twenty-somethings. In her mind's eye, she could see Rye and Max at that age, before the world had tempered them. They would have swaggered through the diner, too, checking out every available female as though it was just a question of which one to choose for the night. If Max's head didn't explode when he caught sight of them, it would be a miracle.

"Hello, darlin'," the shorter one said with a confident smile. Though he was shorter than his brother, he was by no means small. He still had a foot on Rachel. He was definitely the charmer. The taller one was watching her with hooded eyes. He was the broody one.

She smiled back, knowing they were putting on a show that Max and Rye would definitely hear about. "Good evening, gentlemen."

"My name is Shane Kent," the charming one said with a devilish wink. He looked down at her name tag. "And you're Rachel. I like that name, Rachel."

Stella's head came up from her work. She watched the exchange with avid eyes. Rachel knew she would be on the phone talking up the incident the minute she could do so without missing something.

"I'm sure it would suit you. You look like a Rachel," Rachel said saucily. These young men might be good-looking, but they had nothing on Max and Rye. They were puppies compared to her men.

Shane Kent's eyes flared. He looked like a man who liked a challenge. His brother cracked a smile and looked her over with renewed interest. "She's beautiful and funny. I like her. How about you, Bay?"

A long, slow smile crossed Bay Kent's face. "I think she'd suit us just fine, brother."

"How about we take you out tonight, sweetheart?" Shane asked.

"Seriously?" Jen's eyes drifted between Rachel and the brothers. "What kind of perfume are you wearing? Eau de Ménage? Where do I get it?" She shook her head and flounced off.

Rachel wanted to tell Jen that this was all a setup, but she needed the story to get around, and Jen would be very good at doing just that. Stella was already on her cell phone. Rachel bet Teeny and Marie were getting the lowdown.

"Sorry, I already have a boyfriend," Rachel said with a little shrug.

"Only one, darlin'?" Shane asked, his voice smooth as glass. "Why settle for one when you can have two? Trust me, you haven't lived until you've been between us."

Rachel heard every person in the diner draw in a breath. There were a whole bunch of cell phones working overtime now. She had to say that when you wanted word to get out, there was no place better to be than a small town. The gossip grapevine was in full bloom in Bliss. Someone would call Callie Sheppard with the story that Rachel Swift was getting hit on by another set of boys who shared their toys. Rachel was sure Callie would be telling the entire story to Rye within ten minutes.

"I guess I'll just have to take your word for that." Rachel winked at the men and drew her purse over her shoulder. "Good night, boys."

"We'll see you around, Miss Rachel," Bay said slowly.

She felt both of their eyes on her as she walked out of the diner.

The evening air was clean and crisp. Rachel stretched as she walked around the back of the diner to the place where she parked the old Jeep. Max was already making noise about buying her something new. Rachel didn't see the need. Max's car was even older than hers. He'd explained that there was a difference between their vehicles. Max drove a 1976 Ford Ranger, a classic vehicle. Her Jeep was just a piece of junk.

She shook her head as she slipped inside the Jeep. It was true. She'd bought it for $650 off some guy in New Mexico after the unfortunate San Diego incident. It was a jalopy. Sometimes the driver's side back tire got a little low, and it felt that way now. But the ranch was only fifteen minutes outside of town. She could get Max or Rye to air it up for her when she got home. The car started, and the lights worked. That was what mattered. Without another thought about it, she pulled out onto the road and started toward home.

It had only been a week, but those nights she'd spent driving around looking for a safe place to spend the night seemed so far away. She had quickly gotten used to having a place to live and someone to cuddle up with at night while they watched TV. She loved being between the two big men. There wasn't a better way to spend the evening than smooshed between their big bodies. Neither one of them understood the meaning of personal space when it came to her. Even Rye, who, when he thought about it, tried to put some distance between them, ended up touching her when they sat together. The night before, the three of them had sat on the couch and watched a movie. Rachel had been terribly tired. Max offered his shoulder to lean on. Rachel had fallen asleep, and when she'd awakened, her feet were in Rye's lap, being rubbed softly, as though he couldn't help himself. It had been a nice night.

Rachel turned off the main road and onto the little street that led to Harper Stables and some of the other houses both up the mountain and down in the little valley. The stables were down in the valley, but she had to go up to get back down. Max and Rye liked the isolation. Rachel could do without the dirt road. She preferred a nicely paved highway with guardrails. It was a winding road, so she slowed down.

She still wasn't used to driving in the mountains. It always felt like she was too close to the edge. Max drove through this stretch with the casual ease of a local, but it was going to take Rachel time to get used to it. She especially hated driving at night. Though the sun had just gone down, Rachel was already struggling to see.

Suddenly it felt like the entire back end of the car was about to go over the edge. There was a popping sound, and Rachel felt the car swerve. Her hands gripped the steering wheel. She could feel the car start to dangle over the side of the road. It was a long way down. Rachel turned the steering wheel and pressed down on the gas. The wheels spun. The car didn't go anywhere, though. It just made a horrible grinding sound. Rachel's hands were shaking as she cut the engine and engaged the parking brake. Though the car seemed stable, she moved cautiously toward the passenger side. She stepped gingerly out of the vehicle before breathing a sigh of relief. Despite the darkness, she could see the odd way her car was sitting. She was lucky she hadn't gone over the edge.

Rachel pulled out the little cell phone Max insisted she carry. She'd been annoyed at the time, but now she was grateful, or she would be if she could get a signal. There were no bars to be had this high on the mountain. Once she got to the valley, she would be able to make a call. Of course, once she got to the valley, she would be home and wouldn't need to make a call, she grumbled mentally. She pocketed the phone, grabbed her purse, and found a flashlight in the back of the Jeep.

The flashlight told the story. That back tire had finally given up the ghost. It couldn't have picked a worse time. There was no way to change the tire here. She would have to get the Jeep towed. Once that happened, she would never see it again. She knew Max. Max would have a new car shipped in before the old one could get to the shop. She sighed and started to walk.

And really, what was wrong with that? Max wanted her to have a new car. She probably needed one. It worried him every time she drove off. If he needed one and she had the money to buy it for him, she would. Why was she fighting him?

She breathed in the slightly cool night air and knew why. She was afraid. She was afraid of depending on him and Rye. She was terrified it would all go wrong if she let go. It was easier to tell herself that she didn't really need them. They were just fun and sexy. They didn't really matter in the end. She could only count on herself.

The truth was people ran when the going got tough. Rachel had seen it firsthand when Tommy Lane came into her life. When it became obvious she had a crazy stalker in her life, her friends had fallen by the wayside. Some of them had tried to stick it out, but in the end, they had protected themselves. Her best friend Alison's tires had been slashed when Rachel had stayed at her house. Alison had a baby to think about. Rachel didn't really blame Alison for pulling away, but it had taught her a lesson. It was the real reason she hadn't mentioned her little problem to the boys. She was afraid that once they heard about all the trouble following her they would rethink the relationship.

Rachel pointed the flashlight. In the distance she could see the turnoff to Mel's place. There was a light from his cabin. It was so dark here, she thought with a little shiver. The darkness was a soft thing when she was at home, but now it seemed foreboding. That little light in the distance was warm and welcoming.

It was ridiculous. Home was less than half a mile away. She wasn't going to run to the town's craziest conspiracy theorist for protection from the dark. She would walk right past his drive and march straight home.

Rachel heard a sound behind her. She turned and looked back up the road. There was a car coming, but she couldn't see the lights. She heard the car stop, probably taking a look at her own abandoned vehicle. Her car was taking up a lot of the road. It was only natural a local would stop to try to figure out if someone needed help. It could even be Rye coming home, she reasoned and started to turn back.

She stopped. Rye wouldn't be driving without his headlights on. Why would anyone be driving on a dangerous road with their headlights off? Rachel's stomach turned as panic started to take over. Shouldn't the person have called out by now? Whoever was looking over her car was doing it very quietly. She clicked off the flashlight, not wanting to give away her position. In the moonlight she could see the vague outline of a body moving around her car. She would bet it was a man. He was stocky, but then it could be a solidly built woman. There were a whole lot of those around here.

Everything instinct she had told her to run. If he'd found her, there would be no time to rethink her decision. It wouldn't be the first time Tommy had caught up to her. Barely breathing, Rachel started to move off the road onto the grass. She would be quieter there, and she needed to get to Mel's. Mel had a phone, a landline. He thought it was monitored by the alien invasion force, but it worked. She would hole up and call Rye. Her heart was pounding as she watched to see if the shadowy figure was following. All of the terror of the last few years of her life was suddenly riding her hard. She was a mass of survival instincts. Every one of them was focused on one thing, the road in front of her. If everything was all right, then the car would either drive by or someone would call out her name looking for her. Everyone in town knew she drove that Jeep. If everything was all right, she would hear someone yelling for "Rachel," and she would recognize the voice.

Rachel moved behind the tree line as it became clear everything was not all right. There was almost no sound except the dirt crunching as someone walked down the road. Around the corner, a light suddenly came into view. Someone had a flashlight, and he was looking for her.

Without another thought, Rachel ran. She dropped her own flashlight. She simply ran toward the cabin in the distance. She tried to be as quiet as she could, but she was running on adrenaline and panic. Her feet sounded through the woods. She would have sworn she could feel the moment he caught sight of her and began his pursuit.

Rachel turned her head as she ran, trying to catch a glimpse of the man chasing her. She knew who it was. There was no question. He'd found her, and he was going to do what he had always promised. He was going to gut her. He was going to bathe in her blood. Tears were streaming down her face as she prayed to anyone who would listen.

She saw something in the distance, but it was vague and blurry. It didn't matter. She could feel him watching her. She knew he was hunting her. Tree limbs slapped her in the face, but she ignored them. She was wearing a short skirt and sneakers. The brush felt like it was cutting her legs. She kept running. When she stumbled, she popped up as fast as she could, completely ignoring the ache in her knee. None of it would matter if he caught her.

She could hear him moving. He was silent, but in her panic it was as though the very trees were calling her name.

"Liz," she heard them whisper.

But she wasn't Liz anymore, she thought savagely as she ran. She was Rachel. She was stronger than she had been before. He might have her on the run now, but she would get away. She would survive.

She ran into something solid and fell back on her butt. There was a moment of complete terror until she looked up and saw Mel standing over her. He was a slender man, but now he seemed really solid to her in his army fatigues. He held a huge gun in his hands. His eyes were searching the woods. He might be a freaky man, but he was competent with a gun.

"Is it time?" Mel asked, reaching down and hauling her up.

She stood beside him. He pressed something into her hand. It was cold and made of metal. It was a handgun. She immediately flicked the safety off and took a protective stance. She'd learned to use a gun when she realized the cops couldn't protect her. She remembered the day like it was yesterday. She'd been sitting down to lunch when Tommy joined her. He'd told her all the things he intended to do to her if she didn't come back to him. She'd threatened to call the police. He'd simply laughed and told her to prove it. He'd killed her dog the next day, and Rachel had applied for a gun permit.

"Has the invasion started?"

Her voice was shaky as she replied. "No, Mel, I think it's just a man."

"That's what they want you to think," Mel said sensibly. "I just want to know if it's the good guys or the bad guys."

"There are good guys?" Rachel had only heard about the bad ones.

"Oh, sure." Mel was calm and collected as though they were talking about the weather instead of standing at attention with firearms ready to kill anything that moved. "There are some good ones out there. They get lost, or they're on the run from the bad guys. There's always good guys and bad guys, Miss Rachel. That's how the world works." He listened for a moment. "But whoever was out there is gone now."

In the distance, a car drove past. Its lights were on now. She couldn't be sure if it was the same car. Now she felt a little foolish. She hadn't really seen anything except someone checking out a car left on the road. It had probably been spooked campers.

"Why don't you come up to the house?" Mel offered. "I've got some soup, and we can call your men to come get you."

Rachel nodded and started to follow him. She looked back into the woods, but all was silent now.

"And Miss Rachel, I think you should stay away from those Kent boys," Mel said seriously, proving the grapevine worked. "Those two seem like nothing but trouble. I don't think old Max will take kindly to it, and Rye will probably throw them in jail."

The door to Mel's cabin opened. Rachel shook off her panic. She was safe here in Bliss.

# Chapter Twelve

"Where did she go now?" Max turned and looked around the wide, expansive park that housed the picnic grounds. His heart seized a little as he realized he couldn't see Rachel anymore.

"She's with Stella," Rye replied calmly from the ground where he was relaxing. He rested back on his elbows, looking over the crowd. The grounds were covered with people picnicking on blankets, quilts, or making do with the soft grass. There were several tents around the perimeter where people were serving food or offering goods for sale. A large stage was set up at the edge of the park.

Everyone was out for Founder's Day. It was a day to celebrate Bliss's long history and the great men and women who had built the town. No one mentioned that the town had really only been in existence since 1968, when a group of hippies decided it would make a nice commune. Max smiled as he watched Rachel passing out slices of peach pie. His own mama had been one of those hippies. She'd met their dad and become a rancher's wife. Max and Rye had been the first children born in Bliss. His mother would have loved Rachel, Max thought wistfully.

"Rachel would have gotten along great with Mom, you know," Rye said in one of those frequent moments when they were thinking the same thing. Max didn't question it. It was just one of those twin things. It had been like that all their lives. Max felt a little sorry for all the people who didn't have it.

"I'm just glad she seems to get along with Brooke." Max stared at Rachel, wondering just how she'd gotten past Brooke's defenses. Brooke had started talking to Rachel on the phone every couple of days. He knew his baby sister was a hellion. Brooke had scared off more than one female before. She'd been pleased with Rachel, though. She was already talking about making Rachel's wedding dress. Rachel had protested that it was a little early for that. She had no idea that he and Rye were already looking for rings. After Monday, they would make it plain what they needed from her. Max just had to hope she could accept it.

Stefan was stepping up to the stage to announce the next set of auction items. A whole load of local art had already been auctioned off. Some of the local businesses had put items up as well. Stella had offered up a package that included a Pie of the Month membership. The Bliss Repertory Theater had offered season tickets. Henry and Nell had offered performance art lessons. All proceeds would go to the Talbot Foundation, a scholarship program for artists.

Max was getting impatient. He'd come because Rachel had ordered him to. He was anxious to get back to the ranch and work. He wanted to bundle Rachel up and take her back there, too. Last night had just about given him a heart attack. First there had been the moment he and Rye had walked into the diner and realized she wasn't there. After Rye made him calm down, they had started up the route she would have taken to get home. They'd made it to her abandoned Jeep when Callie called over the Bronco's radio telling them Mel had Rachel at his cabin. He owed that crazy and promised to listen to at least one long conspiracy theory a month in payment. He would nod and not interrupt. It was a sacrifice, but well worth it.

Rachel was calm by the time they had gotten to Mel's, but Max knew she'd had a bad night. He'd cradled her while she slept, promising himself that, after Monday, she would still be in his arms.

"Damn, brother," a cocky voice said, "that really is one gorgeous girl."

Max looked up and noted that Rye's attention was now focused on the two young cowboys standing not far from the blanket Rachel had smoothed out for them at the beginning of the picnic. Max grinned.

He remembered what it was like to be twenty-something. He'd been an ignorant ass, too. And he and Rye had had one thing on their minds.

Max looked around, trying to figure out which young lady had caught the brothers' eyes.

"You're right about that," the taller one said. He had his hands on his waist. There was an enormous buckle on his belt proclaiming him the rodeo champion of something or other.

Rye and Max exchanged a look. Max immediately knew these were brothers who shared their toys. He knew his brother was thinking the same thing he was. Those boys were on the prowl, and some lucky woman was in for the ride of her life.

Stefan tapped on the microphone. "Ladies and gentlemen…"

But Max was still watching that younger version of himself. He'd have to point the cowboys out to Rachel. She would find them amusing.

"It's those tits that get me," the shorter one said. "I can't wait to get my hands on them."

His brother smiled as though he was thinking about something very pleasant. "I can't wait to see all that hair spread out. I love that color. Do you think her pussy's strawberry blonde, too?"

"What!" Max yelled, nearly spilling the beer he was holding. It was left on the ground and completely forgotten as he sprang up, realizing those idiots were talking about his woman.

Rye was right beside him.

"Hey, don't spill your beer, old man," the shorter one advised, tipping his Stetson. "You only get so many beers in your life. You gotta enjoy each one."

"Come on, Shane," the other one said. "I think the auction's about to start. I don't want to miss buying up that honey's time."

"Excuse me, sir," the first one said, politely stepping around Rye. "We need to go buy a girl."

They swaggered toward the stage, but Max heard the parting remark. "Nice one, Shane. You're always polite to our elders."

"Elders!" Max shouted. Heads turned, but the younger brothers didn't look back. Max felt his fists clench. They were looking at his woman and talking about her tits. He had kicked ass for far less before.

Rye put a hand out to stop his brother. "Calm down." Rye's eyes were on Rachel as she took off her apron and folded it neatly. "She's a beautiful woman. You can't kick the ass of every man who finds her attractive."

"Watch me," Max growled.

His brother sighed. "Don't embarrass Rachel. You're supposed to be behaving."

Teeny and Marie walked up. Teeny and Marie had been their mother's closest friends. They had been like aunts to the brothers when they were growing up. After their mother had died, it had been Teeny who sat with them at the hospital and Marie who took charge of the arrangements. Their families were interwoven like all the families in Bliss. Brooke had worked at the Trading Post during her teen years, and Teeny's son was Rye's deputy.

"Listen to your brother, Maxwell," Marie admonished. Max looked at the sixty-year-old woman. She was solidly built with a no nonsense air about her. "You calm down. You have bigger things to worry about than those two boys. The whole town knows about Rachel. We're all watching out for her."

Max and Rye had talked to Callie and Logan about getting the word out to the town to watch Rachel. It looked like it worked. Now he had to hope Rachel didn't find out. "Well, while you're all watching out for Rach, I can kill two asshole brothers."

"Those young boys are all arrogance and charm," Teeny said, shaking her head. "You've got nothing to worry about. Rachel turned them down flat last night."

"What?" It was Rye's turn to yelp.

Marie stared at him for a moment. "I thought you would have heard. It was all over town. Those Kent boys came into the diner and asked Rachel out. They said something about two being better than one."

"But Rachel told them she had a boyfriend." Teeny pushed her glasses back up her nose. They were always falling off. She leaned forward conspiratorially. "Stella said they talked about her after she was gone, though. They seemed very interested. They weren't at all concerned that she had a boyfriend."

Max just bet they had talked about her. He should have answered the phone last night. He'd wanted quiet time with Rachel, but from now on, he'd always answer the phone just in case someone was calling to tell him about young men in desperate need of a good ass-kicking.

Rye was looking at the women like he wished they'd be quiet. "Like I told Max, he can't kick the ass of every man who hits on her. Rachel took care of it."

"We have one final item on the block for today's auction," Stefan was saying smoothly.

"See." Rye pointed to the stage. "We're almost done, and then we can take Rachel home. She'll be far away from the lustful gaze of rodeo cowboys."

She might never leave the ranch again. Damn upstart cowboys.

"One of our most beautiful citizens has agreed to auction herself off for an evening," Stefan said with a little laugh. "This will consist of a fantasy date at the Talbot estate. It's an evening of dinner, dancing, and whatever else can happen between consenting adults."

Everyone was chattering about the spicy item up for auction.

"See, I bet they were talking about Jen. Jen's the only one crazy enough to auction herself off." Rye turned his attention to where the Kent brothers were standing near the stage. "They're practically drooling. Stefan's going to get some decent change out of those idiots, and then they'll forget all about Rachel."

"Let me introduce our—" Stefan stopped as a young woman walked up onto the stage. "What should I call you, Rachel?"

She grinned and shrugged. "Let's call me a love slave."

"Excellent." Stefan pushed her gently to the front of the stage. "Do I have a bid on our little love slave?"

"Five hundred dollars," one of the Kent brothers yelled.

Max felt his eye twitching. He knew he should be yelling, but his limbs wouldn't move. This was what it felt like to be paralyzed with rage. Yes, he was going to do it. He was going to finally go utterly psychotic and prove the whole town right. He was going to walk over to those arrogant assholes and take the first one apart. Then he'd beat the other one to death with his dead brother's leg. He looked to his own brother. Rye would save him from his towering rage. Rye would have calming words. Rye would talk him down.

Rye's face was red as he pointed at the young cowboys. "You, kill now, Max."

Max started stalking off toward the idiots trying to buy his woman for the evening. It would be their last evening on Earth.

"Maxwell Harper, you stop right there," Rachel said over the microphone.

"No." Max didn't even slow down as he yelled at Rachel. She wasn't talking him out of it. "I'm going to kill them. They are not going to spend the night with you as their damn love slave."

Rye was right behind him as they bore down on their prey. The Kent brothers stood their ground. Smirks marked their faces as they watched Max and Rye move in.

Max saw Rachel up on stage, tapping that foot of hers. It was one of the things she did when she thought he was acting like a dumbass.

"Well, I was thinking you might buy me, Max," she said with a little huff.

Max stopped. He forgot about the cowboys for a moment. Rachel was staring down at him. "Did you plan this, baby?"

She leaned over, holding her hand over the microphone. It gave him an excellent view of the creamy mounds of her breasts. It also gave the Kent brothers a view. "Yes. I thought it would be fun. I have a whole night planned around being your very obedient little love slave, Max. I know I take control most of the time, but I thought you would enjoy a little obedience from me for once."

His cock got hard at the thought, and he knew Rachel noticed. Damn it. He was going to kill Stefan for letting her do this. It was sweet, and she'd obviously not thought that other men would be bidding. "Fine. Five hundred and one dollars."

It did not go unnoticed that Rachel rolled her eyes at his overwhelming increase.

The Kent brothers laughed, too.

"Six hundred," the one named Shane bid. He winked up at Rachel. "I think you're worth it, darlin'. I'm sure the old man's next bid will be six hundred dollars and fifty cents."

Max growled. He took a step forward, but Rye held him back. Rye looked up at Stefan. "Max will go to a thousand."

Max grimaced, but looked at Rachel, who was waiting expectantly. Her big green eyes were watching him. "Fine."

The Kent brothers grinned. "Two thousand."

Max could hear people talking all around him. He didn't have two thousand. He was building a damn business. He was going to end up in jail because there was no way he would let his Rachel walk off into the sunset to play love slave to two rodeo cowboys.

"Twenty-five hundred," he heard Rye say.

"I thought the other one was bidding," complained one of the Kent brothers.

Stefan looked down from his perch on the stage. "Which one of you is bidding? You should know there's no pooling money. If you do that, then both of you have to share the prize."

"We're more than willing to share." Shane sent a smoldering look Rachel's way. "We heard those two over there don't. We'll show

Miss Rachel a real good time. We're going to show her just how good two men can be."

"Three thousand," Rye shouted. He looked at the younger men. "Three thousand, and I let you live. You go a single dollar over, and all bets are off."

Max took up the topic. His voice was low, so Rachel couldn't hear him. "It won't be a fair fight, boys. You try taking our woman, and you better watch your back the rest of your damn lives. You understand me?"

"I hear you," the tall one said. "As it happens, we could only go to two grand."

Shane sighed. "Damn. I guess we'll have to find comfort elsewhere. You fellas don't happen to have a sister, do you?"

Rye shoved a hand against his brother's chest.

"You stay away from my sister, asshole," Max yelled.

The Kents were laughing as Rye pushed Max away.

"Calm your ass down, Max."

Max looked at his brother, who didn't seem as pissed off as he should be. "Now they're talking about our sister."

Rye looked brutally irritated, but not with the cowboys. "She's safely in Denver, Max. Have you given any consideration to the fact that we just purchased a slave for the night? We just bought a slave for the two of us."

Max's mouth dropped open. He looked up at the stage, where Rachel was talking to Stefan. "She can't know what it means. She was just saying that."

Stefan jogged off the stage as Rachel talked to some blonde who had come with him. She seemed to be giving Rachel very explicit instructions.

Max stopped the elegantly casual Stefan. "This little date I just went into hock for...it's just dinner and stuff, right? She was joking about the slave part."

Stefan frowned. "If she was joking, then Lana wasted an entire morning training her. Rachel was very specific in her demands. She wanted to be a proper slave for the evening. I stocked the guesthouse with everything you could need. There are condoms, lubricant, toys, anything you could want. The hot tub is ready, as well. Dinner will be waiting. She requested that no servants be present, since she intends to be naked the entire time. I do not believe she was joking."

"Damn." Max completely forgot about his need to kick the Kent brothers' young asses. The thought of Rachel naked and submissive to their whims was more than he could comprehend.

"I'll get someone to give me a ride home, brother," Rye said. Max couldn't miss the disappointment in his brother's voice.

"No," Stefan insisted sharply. "I was serious about the rules, Rye. You put in your money, you share the prize."

"That's ridiculous. You can't make her do that."

Stef laughed. "I didn't make the rule, Rye. Rachel did." He slapped Rye on the back. "Take some advice from a man who knows women. She's ready. She wants everything the two of you can give her. Go on and get your woman."

Max and Rye turned to the woman in question. Lana was handing her a key. It was the key to Stefan's guesthouse, where the three of them would come together for the first time.

Max looked at his brother and knew they were thinking the same thing.

About damn time.

# Chapter Thirteen

Rachel took a deep breath as the Bronco came to a stop in front of Stefan Talbot's guesthouse. It was a beautifully constructed cabin with a stark view of the Sangre de Cristo Mountains, but Rachel wasn't thinking of the pretty scenery. The auction had gone poorly. She'd been sure the bidding wouldn't go past five hundred dollars, but that's where those assholes Stef had brought in had started.

She couldn't tell what they were thinking. They had been almost silent since they had collected her from the podium. Max had told her it was time to go. They had waited together while Rye brought the SUV around. She had settled in the back seat before Max could protest, and the ride from the park to Stefan's had been tense to say the least. The men seemed to be on edge.

Rye put the SUV in park and got out quickly. Max opened the passenger door, got out, and then waited on her. His hand squeezed hers as he helped her from the vehicle. She had never been as grateful for anything as she was the feel of Max's arms around her.

"I love you, Rachel," he whispered. He looked at her as though searching for something. "Are you sure, baby? Be sure, because this is forever."

Rachel felt tears threatening. "I love you, Max, but I love Rye, too. Are you all right with that?"

Max's smile held all the warmth of the sun. "Nothing could make me happier."

He held her close, and Rachel felt something deep inside her relax. She wasn't hurting Max.

"But, Rach, you should know, I'm the soft one when it comes to sex. Rye can be demanding."

Rachel felt her eyes widen at that statement. Max was pretty damn demanding himself. Even as she worried a bit about that statement, Rye was proving it to be true.

"Are the two of you done cuddling?" Rye asked in a voice that reeked of authority. "I'd like to go inside and get our evening started."

Rachel nodded and began to walk toward the door. Rye stopped her.

"We need to get a few things straight, Rachel." Rye pulled her close to him. His blue eyes were fierce as he looked down at her. "I want you, Rachel. I love you every bit as much as Max does. If you walk through that door, you will belong to the two of us. Do you understand?"

"I understand that Max wants to marry me." Rachel felt a perverse need to challenge him. He wanted some form of authority over her, but she wasn't giving it to him without some assurances.

Rye's sensual lips turned up as his hands ran down her shoulders. She shivered at the touch. "That's one of the things that attracted me to you, Rachel. You don't sell yourself cheaply. I want commitment from you, too. You'll be legally married to Max because he won the coin toss, but never doubt that you're my wife, too. Do not test me on this, Rachel. If you think Max is a possessive asshole, I have no idea what you'll call me."

She smiled and let her hands find his waist. She let the coin toss statement go. It didn't matter who she legally married. "I'll call you my possessive asshole husband."

He leaned over and, for the first time, pressed his lips to hers. It was short and very, very sweet. "No birth control, Rachel. I want children."

She nodded. She wanted them, too. She had never thought of it before, but now she couldn't imagine her life without their children. They would have curly hair, with red and gold in the brown. They would run rampant across Bliss, Colorado. They would learn how to ride and live in this amazing wilderness that would be their birthright. They would have the best dads in the world.

"Will you marry me, Rachel?" Rye asked plainly.

She nodded, because her heart was far too full for speech.

"Will you marry me, Rachel? Will you be the center of our world and the mother to our children?" Max asked, coming up behind her.

She wrapped one hand behind her around Max's waist, and she was enveloped in them. She was surrounded by the Harper twins. Their warmth and love soothed her soul like nothing had before. Rachel stilled for a moment because she knew she had finally found home.

"Yes," she said simply.

Max kissed her cheek. Rye leaned forward and pressed his lips against her forehead.

Rye was very serious as he spoke to her. Rachel knew he had gotten the formalities out of the way. Now he was ready to get to the sex. "Rachel, do you understand what you agreed to when you put yourself up for auction?"

Her smile was all about seduction now. "Yes, Rye. I did it to tempt you and Max. I wanted to force the situation. I wanted you both."

Max groaned behind her. "And it never occurred to you that saying 'I want you both' might work? We had to give Stef three thousand dollars to get us here."

"I'm so sorry," Rachel said, biting her bottom lip.

Rye backed up. "We'll have the full story later, Rachel. We'll have every story later. Now, I want you to walk through that door. Once you're inside, you'll be our slave. You will follow every order we give you. You will be obedient. Stef said you spent some time with Lana earlier today?"

"When you said you were with Stella?" Max asked.

There was nothing to do but nod.

"She can take her punishment," Rye said in a voice that made Rachel's pussy clench. She wondered exactly what he meant. "Do you understand your role, Rachel?"

"Yes, Rye." She remembered that Lana had said she should use his name or "sir" when she spoke to him.

"Excellent," Rye said, sounding pleased. "Go inside, take off your clothes, and assume the proper position. Max and I will be with you in a moment."

Rachel used the key Lana had given her and practically skipped into the guesthouse. She had no real idea what they were going to do to her, but she knew she would love it. They were hers. The one thing Lana had made clear to her was that that the submissive was really the one in charge. It was her choice to play this role for them. She was more than willing to cede a little sexual power to the two men she loved more than anything. They let her run the show most of the time. She could compromise.

She tossed off her clothes because she had no idea how long they would take to follow her inside. She didn't care if the T-shirt and jeans got wrinkled. She shoved them to the side, then walked to the center of the room. She got on her knees and settled back onto her ankles the way Lana had taught her. She placed her hands palms up on her thighs and waited patiently. It wasn't more than a minute before the door opened, and Max and Rye walked in.

"Very nice," Rye remarked.

She kept her eyes lowered submissively. This wasn't something she would want to do every time they made love, but she could play the role if it made them happy.

"You're beautiful, Rachel," Rye said. She heard the satisfied smile in his voice.

She kept quiet, remembering Lana's training.

"Tell me something, sweetheart," Rye said suspicion plain in his voice. "How long have you known that you wanted the both of us? It occurs to me that you've been very manipulative the last week."

"Hey—" Max attempted to defend her.

"No, Max. Think about it. She's done everything she can to get in between us. She's teased me for a solid seven days. I suspect she knew the effect it was having on me. I want an honest answer, Rachel."

"I knew after Max got shot." If they wanted the story, she would give it to them. "I've been planning this evening for a week. I planned the auction with Stefan."

She heard Rye sigh. "Did he bring in the idiot brothers?"

She bit her lips and went for honesty. "Yes, the older one is an artist. I never meant for it to get so expensive."

Max growled. "He better buy them a one-way ticket out of town, or those boys are in for the ass-kicking of a lifetime."

Through her lashes, she saw they were efficiently getting undressed. Rye shoved his jeans off his hips. Her mouth watered as she took in the sight of Rye Harper's enormous cock. It shot straight up his abdomen, easily reaching his navel. His cock was hard and ready. Max was ready, too, Rachel noted as he tossed his shirt aside and handily rid himself of his denims. Max's eyes gleamed down at her as he sat back in a chair. He lounged, heedless of his nudity. His big hand stroked his cock slowly. He was just warming up. He could stroke himself for a long time.

Suddenly Rye was standing before her.

"Look up, Rachel." His blunt tone told her everything she needed to know. He was on edge. Rachel knew she was going to have to take that edge off if she wanted the evening to go well. She'd pushed Rye hard this week, and he seemed to be feeling the effects.

Rachel obediently turned her eyes up. "Yes, Rye?"

"I like this game, Rach." He touched her chin with his index finger. He tipped her head up so she faced him. "I learned from the best."

"Stef?"

His finger covered her lips. "I'll let you know when you can talk."

That rankled, but she kept quiet.

Rye chuckled. "I'll pay for this later, baby. I know that. You're not exactly a submissive girl. Play my games, and I'll play yours. How about that?"

Rachel kept silent, but let her smile show through her eyes. Rye seemed satisfied with that.

"Now, Max, you've been fucking this sweet woman of ours for weeks now," Rye started.

"Not nearly as often as I'd like," Max replied smoothly. He looked content, to Rachel's relief. He looked happy to be here. Any fears she had that Max didn't want to share were gone now.

Rye just looked hungry. Rye's entire body was coiled and ready to pounce. "How's her mouth?"

Max groaned. The head of his cock was weeping now. "She gives amazing head. She can suck you dry. I'd fuck that mouth of hers if I were you."

Rye took himself in hand. Suddenly that big cock of his was requesting entrance. "Open up, sweetheart." He didn't wait for her to comply. He teased her lips with the bulbous head of his cock.

Rachel opened and let her tongue find the little V on the underside of his dick. She lathed it with the tip of her tongue.

"Lick the head," Rye growled.

Rachel swirled her tongue around the purple head of his cock. She could already taste the pre-cum leaking from the slit. She lapped it up and let it coat her tongue, reveling in the taste of him. She sucked just the head of him into her mouth and tugged lightly.

"Fuck this, I can't wait." Rye groaned as he pulled back. He wound a hand through her hair. "I'm going to fuck your mouth, sweetheart, and when you're done sucking me dry, you're going to crawl over to Max on your hands and knees. You're going to suck him dry, too. We're both going to use that pretty mouth of yours, and you won't lose a drop of what we give you. Do you understand?"

Rachel nodded. Then Rye was slowly, steadily feeding her his hard length. She struggled to open her jaw up.

"Relax, Rachel," he ordered as he filled her mouth. Rachel concentrated on breathing through her nose. "Use your hands to cup my balls. I like having my balls played with. Remember that."

She reached up and gently cupped his heavy, tight sac. He groaned with pleasure and shoved another inch in. Rachel could feel him hitting the back of her throat with each little thrust. She managed to run her tongue along the underside of his dick, causing him to hiss.

"Fuck, that feels good, Rach." The hand in her hair tightened as he picked up the pace. "Your mouth feels like heaven. Suck me hard. I'm going to come. I can't last."

Rachel hollowed out her cheeks and sucked his dick rhythmically. He seemed to lose control. He started to fuck her mouth hard. He pushed his dick in as he tugged on her hair, pulling her forward. She was filled with him, and Rachel gave up control, letting him use her mouth. She relaxed. He fucked his way to the back of her throat. When she felt his head bump as far as he could go, she swallowed around him. She squeezed his balls gently.

"Fuck," Rye shouted as he started to come. Rachel felt him tense, and then she thought of nothing but swallowing the cum shooting out of his cock. She swallowed furiously, not letting an ounce go.

As he softened in her mouth, Rye continued to hold her on his dick. "Lick it all up, baby." His voice was ragged. His hands loosened in her hair, smoothing it lovingly. When he seemed satisfied she'd taken everything he'd given her, he pulled out of her mouth with an audible pop. He tugged on her hair, forcing her to look up at him.

Rachel could tell he wasn't anywhere close to complete satisfaction. He would want more.

"Now, before you go over there and run that hot little tongue all over Max's cock, I want to see my pussy."

"What?" Rachel asked. She breathed deeply, forcing the air into her lungs.

"I said I want to see my pussy. Lay back, spread your legs, and let me look at my pussy."

"He's not kidding, baby," Max said with a husky laugh. "He really wants to just look at it. He'll make you spread your legs for him at least once a day so he can look at you."

Rye stared at her. Nothing in his gorgeous face gave her a hint that he was joking. "I'm waiting."

Rachel nodded and got up off her knees. She sat down on the carpeted floor and slowly spread her legs. She knew she should be terribly self-conscious, but the lust and love in their eyes made her feel utterly wanton. She felt beautiful, and she wanted to share that with them.

Max leaned forward, his eyes wide. "When did you shave?" He was breathless. He focused on her plump, ripe, completely hairless mound.

"I waxed this morning." It had been part of the ritual Lana had put her through. She'd screamed a little during the actual process, but was pleased with how soft and sensitive she was down there.

"It's gorgeous," Max breathed.

"Spread the lips." Rye's cock was growing already. It was pulsing with need again as he watched her. "Use your fingers and spread your lips. I want to see your little clit. I want to know if you're creamy and ripe."

She was. She'd had to change underwear twice before the picnic just thinking of what would happen. Now that she was here and they were naked, she couldn't stop her pussy from creaming. She ran her fingers between her labial lips and parted them as Rye requested. Her fingers were slick as they became coated in her arousal. She nearly cried out as she brushed the pink pearl of her clitoris. She was close. All it would take was a few strokes of her finger to send her over the edge.

"Don't you dare touch that again." Rye reached down and took her hand. He pulled her up and into his arms. His erection pressed into the soft flesh of her abdomen. She wanted it somewhere else. "That pussy is mine, Rachel. It belongs to me and Max. You leave it alone until I tell you to touch it. Do you understand?"

She nodded. Later on, she'd call him on his hypocrisy, but saucy answers had no place in the here and now. She'd agreed to play the submissive and intended to stick to it. Later on, she promised herself, she and Rye would have a long discussion about his masturbatory practices. That possessiveness was going to work both ways.

Rye reached down between them and slid a strong finger through the slick folds of her pussy. Rachel panted as he played for a minute. His talented fingers danced around her clit, tantalizing her but never quite shoving her over the edge. He dipped his middle finger into her juicy cunt and then, to Rachel's dismay, pulled his hand away. He brought his soaked fingers to his mouth and sucked the juice off his hand.

"She tastes like honey," Max said, leaning back. He was relaxed and waiting his turn.

"She is sweet." Rye savored her cream. "I'll eat that pussy later, Rachel. For now, you have something to do to Max, if I recall. Hands and knees."

Rachel dropped to the floor. She began to crawl toward Max, who watched her with hooded eyes. He sat in a comfortable overstuffed chair. Rachel heard Rye leave the room, but focused her attention on Max. He looked so scrumptious waiting for her. His strong jawline sported the five o'clock shadow he always seemed to have. She loved how masculine he was.

He spread his legs wide, giving her plenty of room to work. He stroked his long dick. His eyes were hot as she licked him from his wide base all the way to the head. She worked slowly. She knew Max got a lot of his pleasure from watching. He wanted to see his cock sinking into her. Max relaxed back in the chair. He allowed her to do the work.

She licked him like a lollipop, one hand stroking the shaft as she devoured the head. It was work she could get used to.

* * * *

Rye walked back into the living room and was greeted with the gorgeous sight of Rachel's ass swaying as she slowly, lovingly ate Max's cock. His own cock tightened again at the thought of how hot that mouth had been. Rachel was small compared to him, but she was potent. He'd loved the fact that he almost couldn't fit in her tight little mouth. She'd been so small that he'd felt the edge of her teeth scraping gently along his flesh. It had just made him come harder.

She was so fucking gorgeous, Rye thought as he opened the bottle of lubricant he'd found beside the bed. It wasn't the only thing he'd found in there. Stef had left a bounty for them to play with, each toy brand new and ready for use. He looked down at the pink plug in his hand. It was small, but it would look so luscious clenched in her tight little asshole. His cock jumped. He knelt down behind her and rubbed his hands along the curves of her ass. He couldn't help himself. He leaned over, kissing each plump, round cheek. He worshipped her. Rachel murmured softly around the cock in her mouth and wiggled her backside, inviting him to play.

That was an invitation he would never refuse. He squirted a little of the pre-warmed lubricant onto his hand and gently parted her cheeks.

"Have you fucked this tight little ass, yet, Max?" Rye asked, watching his brother. Max's head was back and his eyes closed as he gave himself up to Rachel's mouth. Rye knew it wouldn't be long before Max filled her with cum for the second time tonight.

"Not yet." Max moaned as Rachel sucked him deep. "I've been playing around. She likes it."

Rachel muttered something that might have been a yes. Rye used his middle finger to slowly work the lube into her clenching anus. He massaged the pretty hole and thought about how good it would feel wrapped around his dick. He lubed up the plug and pressed it to her backside. There was a second's hesitation.

"You press back when I tell you to, Rachel. I'm going to fuck your little ass with this plug. It will get you ready for my dick." Every word he said was a promise he made to her, to himself. Max might have had her first, but Rye was taking her virgin ass.

He pushed forward and watched her little anus clench trying to keep him out. He pushed in, gently rotating. "Press against it, baby."

Rachel groaned as she pressed back against him. He slipped in past the tight ring of muscles.

"She's ready for it, Max." Rye's voice was guttural to his own ears. "We can fuck her together tonight."

He eased the plug out and then back in. Rachel's body trembled. She whimpered sweetly around Max's cock. It made Rye think all sorts of dark things. He shuddered at the thought of reaming her ass with his cock.

"I planned on it," Max groaned.

Rye noted that Max was giving up on his previous "lay back and enjoy" state of mind. His jaw was tense, and his hips thrust up as he fucked into Rachel's mouth. Rye knew his brother was going to blow soon. He remembered all too well how good it felt to bump the back of her throat as she swallowed him down. She was a tremendously giving lover.

Rye fucked her with the plug. His dick pulsed as he watched the pink plastic toy disappear into her hole. The puckered ring of muscles tightened and relaxed over and over as he worked her. She was tentative at first, but after a minute or two she was pushing her ass back on the plug. She was practically begging for it.

"You like this," Rye heard himself saying. "You like having your ass fucked. How much better is it going to be when it's my cock, Rach? Are you going to love it when my cock is up your ass and Max is fucking your pussy?"

She was moaning, shoving her ass against the plug. Rye couldn't wait a minute longer. He pushed the plug in, fitting it tightly in her ass. He left it there. It was so pretty. His cock was going to explode if he didn't fuck her soon.

Her thighs were covered in her arousal. She'd loved having her ass used. Before the night was over, she'd take way more than the little plug, but now Rye wanted to know what it was like to sink into her cunt.

"Spread your legs, gorgeous," he ordered. He lined his dick up to her slit.

Rachel moaned as she tried to force her pussy onto his cock.

Rye smacked her pretty ass. Rye liked the way her skin pinkened. A gush of fresh cream coated him. "Don't lose Max, or I'll have to punish you, baby."

"Yes," Max said. He sounded a little desperate. "Don't lose Max. Suck me, baby. I'm so close." He drew her head back down. Rye soon heard the sweet sound of her slurping and sucking.

"Get Max to give you his cum, and I'll ride you." Rye ran his hands along her curves. He let his dick sink in just a touch to give her something to think about. It was so tempting to just shove his way in. Rachel was so wet, he would slide right in.

"Oh, Rachel," Max moaned. His face flushed, and he gritted his teeth. His hands tightened around her hair, and his hips pumped. "Baby, that feels so good. Swallow me."

Rachel sucked deeply, and Max's face flushed and contorted as he filled their woman's mouth with his cum.

When Max laid back, utterly spent, Rye went to work. He pulled Rachel back onto his cock. He pushed in all the way to his balls. Her slick pussy walls sucked at him, pulling him in and tightening all around him. The plug in her ass made her cunt ridiculously tight. He groaned at the exquisite feel of her pussy. He pulled out, guiding her with his hands. When he pulled back, he could see the pink plug peeking out from between the cheeks of her ass, and he lost it. He plunged in hard and fast. He couldn't help it. He'd waited weeks for this. Hell, he'd waited all of his life to find her.

"Oh, Rye, please fuck me." She was on her hands and knees thrusting back against him. He loved the way she moved and the sound of flesh slapping against flesh. He moved his hands from her hips to her breasts. They swayed in time to the rhythm of their fucking. He plucked at the nipples, pinching and twisting them just enough to let her feel it. "It feels so good. Fuck me hard, Rye."

He smiled, because that was not the plea of a submissive woman. It was a woman demanding her pleasure, and he was a man who would give it to her. Rye liked to play games, but he wanted Rachel just the way she was. He wanted her fighting Max and telling him what to do and where to stick it when she got pissed. He needed her passion and strength. As he gave her what she wanted, Rye knew he would love her forever.

He pulled his hands back up to grip her thighs. He pounded her pussy, pulling and pushing her whichever way he wanted. She was his. The friction and the heat of her cunt were pushing him over the edge far too soon. Rye felt a little shiver at the base of his spine, and his balls drew up painfully. He groaned because there was no way he could hold off any longer. She was too tight and too wet. Her pussy sucked at his cock, milking him. Rye reached around and his hand slid through her juice. He found that little button that was sure to set Rachel off. He firmly pressed his finger against her clit as he ground his cock into her one last time. Rachel shuddered, and he felt her come. She said his name over and over. She spasmed around him, her little muscles clenching at him. He practically saw stars as he poured himself into her.

He was shaking as he slumped forward onto Rachel's back. She fell into Max's lap. Max immediately began stroking her hair. His brother told their woman how beautiful she was and how happy they were to have her. He was glad Max had the words to express how they felt because they failed Rye. Rye lay against her, breathing in her scent and listening to the sound of her thundering heart.

# Chapter Fourteen

Rachel held on to Max as he carried her through the cabin, back toward the bedroom. Rachel knew what was waiting for her there. There was a king-sized bed with one-thousand-thread-count sheets and just about every sex toy known to man. She squirmed a little in Max's arm trying to adjust to the toy Rye had shoved up her ass not ten minutes before. Every time she moved, the little plug sent mini-shocks through her entire lower body. When Lana had shown her the room earlier in the day, she'd wondered if Stefan Talbot had his own manufacturing company that specialized in the truly filthy. There were dildos, butt plugs, feathers, various things that vibrated, lubricants in assorted flavors, and the list went on and on. She didn't even know what some of the things did. There was an odd bench that seemed too low to really aid in reaching high places. It almost looked like a mini picnic table. Rachel stared at it for a moment.

"What are the little hook things for, Max?" Rachel asked curiously. Her arms were draped around his broad shoulders, and she sounded slightly sleepy even to her own ears. She was strangely fascinated by the decadent space Stefan called his "playroom." Rachel noted that Rye had one of the closet doors open and was looking for something. None of them was wearing a stitch of clothing. Rye's muscled backside was completely bare, and that was how she liked it.

"That's for the handcuffs or rope or whatever your master chooses to tie you down with," Max replied with a salacious grin on his handsome face. He looked awfully naughty to Rachel.

"What?" Rachel looked at the little stool again. "Why would you want to handcuff me to a stool?"

"It's called a whipping chair, and it's all the better to spank you with, my dear." There was a distinctly wolfish leer on Rye's face. He held a leather riding crop in his hand. He tapped it against his palm as though testing it.

Rachel narrowed her eyes and gave him her stare. It was the one that let the Harper twins know that they could probably get her to do something, but they would pay for it later.

Rachel was satisfied when Rye took one look at her, gulped, and put the crop back in its storage place. "No crop for you, then. You would probably use it on me later."

"You smack my ass with that or that paddle thing with the holes, and, yes, there will likely be retribution," Rachel replied as Max set her on the bed. He tossed her down and followed quickly, rolling with her. His hands were everywhere, playing with her boobs, caressing her backside, and tickling the backs of her knees.

Rye closed the door, and turned back to them. He had something in his hands, but it looked like jewelry rather than a crop or a paddle. His lips were in a half smile as he stared down at them. Rachel gasped as Max caught a nipple between his teeth and bit down gently.

"What happened to my little submissive?" Rye asked wistfully.

Rachel frowned. She wasn't very good at this. "I'm sorry, Rye. You're right." She managed to get up despite Max's protests. She turned. She got onto her hands and knees, presenting her bottom to Rye. If he wanted to explore a little light spanking, then she could try. "If you want me to get onto the bench thingie, I will."

Rye laughed, and his big hands caressed her ass lovingly. He pressed in on the plug, making her moan and writhe. Max repositioned himself, and his hands found her breasts. He plucked at the nipples while his mouth lightly nipped the back of her neck. Rachel sighed at the sensation. Her pussy was heating up again. She couldn't believe how hot these men could get her.

"Show me your breasts, Rachel." Rye's deep voice stroked across her skin.

She came up on her knees and turned to Rye.

Max gave her a hot wink as she glanced at him. "Show him those tits, baby. They are so pretty."

She let her hands cup her breasts offering them up for Rye's delectation. She was rewarded with a slow curving of his lips.

"Max got those nipples hard, didn't he? You can get them harder though, can't you, brother?"

Suddenly Max's hands came around her back. She could feel his erection pressing into her backside. His fingers pushed hers aside and took their place at her breasts. His big hands cupped her breasts, massaging and stroking them. She let her head fall back against Max's chest. He pinched her nipples between his thumb and forefinger.

"They're tight, Rye. Put those jewels on our little doll now." Max's deep rumble brought her back to attention. She looked up, and Rye was reaching for her.

"She is our little doll. I think I'll dress her up." Rye had what looked like long, jeweled earrings in his hands.

"What is it?" Rachel asked.

"Max, spank that ass." Before Rye could get the words out, Max's hand came down sharply on her ass, and she yelped at the little sting. The slap moved the plug, making every nerve in her backside come to life. The stinging pain on her skin was quickly replaced with a light heat that she felt in her womb.

"I think we'll just use our hands, baby." Rye chuckled. His voice was low and sexy. "I don't think we need to bring a crop or a whip into it. There are too many places for you to actually get your hands on a riding crop. I don't think I'd like where you would shove it. Now, I didn't tell you it was time to talk, but I'll answer your question anyway. This, baby, is a nipple clamp, and it is going to look so pretty on those tits of yours."

He opened the clamp and fitted it to her nipple. The clamp bit into her sensitive flesh. Like the plug in her ass, it was on just the right side of pain. She hissed as he clamped her other nipple and sat back.

"Very pretty. Those will jiggle nicely when we fuck you hard. Now, hands and knees, Rachel." Rye's cock was jutting out from the V of his thighs. Rachel wanted it in her mouth, but she went to her knees in front of him.

"She's very obedient," Max said. His hand traced the line of her spine. They took up places of either side of her body.

"Now she is, but she has a lot to make up for." Rye's hand came down on her ass.

Rachel couldn't stop the moan that came from the back of her throat. Maybe the spanking thing wasn't so bad.

Rye continued, "Our little woman is never going to be submissive, Max. We have to be very careful. I think she might take some creative revenge if we get too extreme. See, Rachel, if I use my hand, then the only revenge your little heart is going to be able to have on me is slapping your hand against my ass." She felt his lips kissing where he had spanked. "And, Rachel, your hands are welcome on my ass anytime."

"Mine, too," Max said sweetly. His face came into view as he lay down underneath her. Rachel was struck at how open and happy Max looked. The bear of Bliss County looked sweet and sexy. "You can spank me anytime you like. You just tell me to get on your lap, and I'll count it out, baby."

Rachel snorted at the thought. It turned into a little squeal as Rye smacked her again. This whole not talking thing was getting to her.

"Go on and say what you need to say." Rye let her off the leash.

"Don't tempt me, Maxwell. You know you deserve it sometimes." Rachel was pretty sure there were citizens of Bliss who would pay good money to watch her tan Maxwell Harper's hide.

"And I'll take it," Max replied with a wink. "I just get to call you Rachel, Mistress of Pain whenever you discipline me. I'm likely to do bad things just so you'll punish me."

Rye's hand came down right in the center of her ass. She gritted her teeth against the sensation. The plug jerked in her ass, a jumble of pain and wild pleasure. The clamps on her nipples were heavy, pulling at her, tugging. The heat bloomed outward, a sweet feeling that made her restless. She leaned down and pressed her lips to Max's. His tongue reached out to touch hers.

"You don't need a reason," she said. "You'll do bad things because you're Maxwell Harper."

He didn't try to protest. "Yes, but the discipline is an added incentive to misbehave." He winked at her, and his face disappeared. She felt him moving behind her. She tried to look back.

"Eyes front, Rachel," Rye ordered.

Rachel gamely turned back. She stared at the carved wooden headboard, but her mind was on the two men now running four hands all over body. She breathed slowly, trying to calm down her racing heart. It felt like there was no place she wasn't being worshipped by their hands. They didn't leave an inch of her skin untouched. Fingers plucked at the clamps on her nipples, and a warm tongue ran down the length of her spine. Someone nipped firmly at the hollow of her ankle. She was shocked at how sensitive she was there. The Harper brothers were finding all her hot spots. They were finding some she didn't even know she had.

She nearly protested when she felt one of them leave the bed, but then she heard Rye's voice and felt his hands on her thighs. "Spread your legs, darlin'." He growled the command. She felt him slide his shoulders between her splayed legs. "I want access to my pussy."

Max's weight was back on the bed. She felt his hands spreading the cheeks of her ass. "I'm going to take out this plug and work some more lube into your ass, baby," Max said matter-of-factly. "Then, I'm going to fuck you with a bigger plug. I want to make sure you're ready to take me and Rye there. You understand how we want to fuck you, right?"

She nodded as she bit her lip against the slight burning sensation. She breathed out as he pulled out the plug. There was a sense of relief, and a strange feeling of disappointment. She'd been so full. Max was rubbing her with the lube, working it into her anus. He rimmed her over and over. It made her eyes water and every nerve a little jittery. It was a very intimate sensation. "One in my pussy, one in my ass." She'd thought of nothing else for the last week.

"That's right." Rye's warm breath was right over her pussy. It was all she could do not to shove herself onto his face. She felt his tongue reach up to delicately lap at her labia.

"Oh, please, Rye." She wanted him to fuck her with his tongue. She could feel the flexible plastic head of the plug begin to breach her anus. It was so much bigger than the first one. It was probably still smaller than Max and Rye.

"We're going to stuff you full of our cocks." Max was breathing heavily as he slowly pushed the plug into her ass. "When you think you can't handle any more, baby, that's when we ride."

Her head fell forward. The twin sensations of burning pleasure and the delicate feel of Rye gingerly stroking her with his tongue were making her crazy. The jewels on her breasts jangled. It felt like every nerve in her body was being manipulated by them.

"Rye, please," she pleaded again. The plug was all the way in now. She felt the muscles in her ass working to accommodate the larger plug. Max pulled the plug in and out, fucking her ruthlessly.

"Was there something you wanted, Rachel?"

Rye sounded entirely too calm for her peace of mind. She was nearly senseless with desire. She needed them so much. "You know what I want."

"Then let me hear you say it." His breath floated across her pussy like a warm blanket.

"Eat my pussy, Rye." She gave him the words he wanted. Max slowly pulled the plug out and then carefully began pushing it back in. The pressure was going to kill her. She needed to come.

His tongue just barely touched her clitoris. "What do think I'm doing, darlin'?" He pressed little kisses along her labia.

"Teasing me." He was going to drive her insane. He was acting like a cat lapping up cream. She needed more than the slow, tantalizing tongue-lashing he was giving her.

She hissed as he very gently bit down on her clit.

Max pulled the plug out of her ass. "Are we going to do this, or are you just going to torture her the rest of the night?"

"It would serve her right," Rye said. Rachel could feel him smiling against her skin. His tongue ran lightly over her heated flesh.

"You're torturing me, too," Max grumbled.

Rye chuckled, and Rachel felt his hands on her hips. "Fine. Sit on my face, baby. I'll eat your pussy."

He pulled her down, and Rachel was suddenly on her knees with her butt against Rye's sculpted chest. Her head fell back as Rye shoved his tongue up her cunt, urging her to move against him. His strong tongue pushed into her pussy. He licked and sucked at her soaking flesh. He fucked deeply into her, his fingers pulling her pussy lips apart so he could get as far inside her as he could go.

Max moved in front of her, watching the scene with hot eyes. He leaned in and kissed her while she ground her pussy against his brother's mouth, riding his tongue.

"I love these tits," he breathed into her ear. "Look at how they bounce. So fucking pretty. Let's see how you like this." He pulled gently on the nipple clamps. She gasped as the sensation went straight to her pussy.

Rye's hands parted her as his tongue swiped across her clit. It set off a wave. The heat and pressure started in her pussy, but it bloomed across her skin. Her head fell back as she came. Max milked her nipples, and Rye tortured her clit until she sobbed and came again.

She shook as Max pulled her off his brother's mouth and rolled across the bed with her. She was still experiencing little aftershocks as Max settled her over him.

"Ride me." He groaned as he pushed his way into her.

Rachel let herself sink slowly onto his cock. Her body was still humming from the orgasms they had already rung out of her. She wasn't sure she could take another, but she couldn't deny them. She watched Max's eyes. He didn't take them off the sight of his big dick disappearing slowly into her pussy. His face strained with the effort he was putting forth. He held himself still and let her control the pace. Rachel could see how much it was costing him.

A big hand caressed her back. "Lean forward, Rachel. This virgin ass is mine."

Rye moved in behind her. She couldn't see him, but knew he must be between Max's legs. He gently urged her forward.

Max steadied her against his arms. The look of love and lust in his eyes reassured her more than words could. She tensed as she felt the head of Rye's cock start to push into her ass.

"Relax, baby," Max whispered. "Let us take you. It's going to be so good. You'll be so full."

Rye's dick was far bigger than anything that had breached her tight hole previously. She gritted her teeth and hissed as he patiently worked his way in. The pressure burned.

"She is so fucking tight." Rye groaned behind her. His hands gripped her hips and pulled her back with ruthless intent. "Shove back against me, baby."

She took a deep breath, then did as he asked. Making sure to not lose Max, she carefully pushed her backside toward Rye. She gasped as she felt his cock push past her asshole, and he shouted as he breached her.

"Oh, God, Rachel, you feel so good. Do you have any idea how hot you are?" Rye sounded like a man in pain.

"I know how hot she is." Max thrust up, and Rachel groaned. She could feel her nails digging into Max's flesh. Max was staring over her shoulder with an impatient look on his face. "Are you ready to fuck or not?"

Rye thrust in, and she could feel his balls hit the cheeks of her ass. "Let's ride."

Rachel had never felt so full in her life. She could barely breathe. When Max stroked in, Rye retreated. He pulled himself almost all the way out of her sensitive ass only to tunnel ruthlessly back in. Every nerve in her body was singing. She felt like she was riding a giant wave that pushed her back and forth, but it didn't matter because any way she went felt incredible. She felt Rye pounding into her, all delicacy gone now. Max's hips slammed up, and his hands pulled her down at the same time. She thought she was going to faint when Max reached out and firmly stroked her clit. Rachel went flying. Anything she knew before went right out the window. This was so far past any orgasm she'd ever had. This was a bomb going off in her body. She screamed as Rye stiffened behind her. Hot cum filled her ass and then her pussy as Max gave in, too.

She fell forward into Max's arms, his cock still tucked into her body. Rye gently pulled out of her ass and rolled to the side.

"I love you, Rachel," he whispered. His mouth caressed her forehead.

She slipped off Max's body and found herself nestled in between them. She laid her head down on Max's chest. Rye's arm slipped around her waist.

"I love you," she replied sleepily. Her body still hummed. "I love you both."

She fell asleep feeling safer than she ever had before.

\* \* \* \*

Deep in the night, Tommy Lane watched the three lovers cavort in a hot tub. If he thought he could get away with it, he would march across the yard and drive a knife into all three of their hearts.

What a whore she had turned out to be, Tommy fumed. He had to take a deep breath before he pulled the binoculars back up to his face. She held out on him, but she gave it up for two brothers. It was disgusting. It had been bad when he thought she was fucking around with one of the twins. Now he could see what a piece of trash she was.

They passed her between them like a toy they were playing with. It made him sick. Liz, that slut, was laughing and kissing them in turn. She was such an idiot. They were just screwing around with her. Those two cowboys would kick her to the curb when they were finished because that was what you did with a piece of garbage.

He would have treated her right. Women couldn't see a good thing when it stood in front of them. But he would show her. He would stand in front of her, and he would show her the mistake she had made. She would beg him for forgiveness before she died.

Liz's laughter rang across the yard. It made his hands twitch. He wanted them wrapped around the bitch's throat. He wanted to watch her cry and plead. He wanted to see that moment when she realized he had no mercy. That was the moment he was waiting for. It was the moment when he would feel like the king of the world.

She threw her head back. It was obvious she was fucking one of the brothers. The other one sat back and watched.

Tommy threw the binoculars down and barely contained his scream of rage.

He wouldn't watch any more. He turned to walk back through the woods. He hated this fucking place. It was full of weirdoes and perverts. He stalked back to where he had left his truck, thinking about how she had made it here.

He'd tracked her to San Diego roughly six months before. Before he started dating a woman, he always did his research. It was best to go into a situation with the upper hand from the get-go. Before he even met her, he'd known where she worked, where she lived, how many parking tickets she had, and who she hung out with. He had certainly checked on her family. The fact that she didn't have parents or siblings to deal with had made her all the more appealing to Tommy. Liz Courtney had one relative in the world, an elderly aunt. He knew from her coworkers that Liz contacted her once a week. He couldn't imagine Liz dumping old Auntie Sadie just because she was on the run. It was just a matter of time before she showed up there. Especially after the old girl fell down some stairs and died. He grinned in the darkness, remembering how the old lady had begged him to call an ambulance. She'd been a tough old broad, but they all died in the end.

He'd been waiting when Liz showed up to say goodbye to her last relative. At the time, her hair had been auburn, but he'd known it was her right away. She couldn't hide from him. But she'd slipped through his fingers. She was quicker and more attentive than he'd expected her to be. She must have caught sight of him watching her at the funeral home. He'd waited, but she'd never come back out. Somehow she'd gotten past him, and by the time he saw her sedan flying down the road, it was far too late. She'd changed her name again.

Tommy got into his truck and started the engine. He'd been a little more creative this time. It hadn't taken a genius to know that Liz had help running. She wasn't smart enough to do it on her own. One of his cop buddies remembered that the nurse on Liz's floor had lost her daughter years before. All it took was simple surveillance to discover she was quite the little helper of "downtrodden women." Once he knew who her source was for fake IDs, it had been simple to ferret out what names Liz would use. He'd started looking for Shannon Matthews and Rachel Swift immediately.

He couldn't believe it when he heard someone from a podunk Colorado town was looking for information on one Rachel Swift. The cop community was small, and despite the internal affairs investigations into him, Tommy maintained his friendships. It served him well, as he'd found her and intended to take care of the problem once and for all.

Tommy thought about those damn brothers as he turned his car toward their ranch. It was obvious they were holed up with Liz for the night at the rich guy's place. Tomorrow they would come home, and Tommy would have a surprise waiting for them. He wouldn't underestimate any of them this time. Shooting the first brother hadn't worked. Making sure Liz's tire blew out hadn't worked, either. He'd gotten there moments too late. When he'd chased after her, she'd managed to find some idiot with a flipping AK-47. He shook his head. The whole town was freaking nuts, and he was pretty sure they all had guns.

It didn't matter. After tomorrow, Liz would be dead. Those brothers would be gone, too. They should enjoy the night together. It would be their last.

# Chapter Fifteen

Rachel woke up to the sound of shouting. She tried to snuggle back under the warmth of the comforter but was disconcerted to find herself alone. When she'd been allowed to sleep, she'd slept wrapped in their arms. Rachel was rapidly getting used to cuddling.

"Fuck you, Stef!" Max yelled. His voice pulled her roughly from her attempt to get back to sleep.

"I can't believe you're yelling at me." Stefan's voice was calmer than Max's, but it rang across the yard all the same. "You got exactly what you wanted."

Rachel opened her eyes and saw Rye kneeling on the bed. He was looking out the window behind the big king-sized four-poster bed. "Is Max making an ass of himself?" Her voice was husky with sleep. It was fitting. She hadn't gotten much sleep last night. Max and Rye had been incredibly demanding. She was sore, but she already felt her body heating up at the sight of Rye's gorgeous backside. He hadn't bothered with clothes.

"I think this is going to be a spectacular scene, darlin'." He reached down and helped her up. "Really, you shouldn't miss it."

Rachel rubbed her eyes and watched as Max stalked after their host. Stefan was already a vision of elegant masculinity in a dress shirt, slacks, and shoes that were probably worth a fortune. Max, on the other hand, only had on a worn pair of Levi's. His hair was slightly unkempt. His six-pack was on heart-stopping display. He looked delicious.

"You manipulative son of a bitch," Max growled. "How dare you go behind my back and talk my woman into doing something as stupid as auctioning herself off in front of the whole town!"

"I didn't think it was stupid," Rachel muttered.

Rye patted her ass comfortingly. "I thought it was a brilliant plan."

She smiled, remembering how pissed he'd been at the time. One night of incredibly indulgent sex seemed to have done wonders for Rye's mood. She filed that information away for future reference. When Rye got upset with her, she'd take him to the bedroom and end the argument.

"How do you know it wasn't Rachel's idea in the first place?" Stefan crossed his arms over his chest. His handsome face was contorted into an expression that conveyed his general annoyance.

"Because she is a sweet girl," Max proclaimed righteously. "She is just a little naïve. You used her."

Rachel shook her head. "Naïve?"

Rye shrugged. "I was going to take issue with sweet."

She elbowed him playfully.

"I want my three thousand dollars back," Max shouted.

Even from a distance, Rachel could see Stefan rolling his eyes. "You cheap son of a bitch. You think I don't know how much you have in the bank? You might not be rich, but you're not going to starve. That money went to charity. You're not getting it back. Besides, you only chipped in a grand. I hope Rye got two-thirds of the sex last night."

Max stood his ground. His body was tense, and he looked ready to attack. "You tell me something, Stef. Did you or did you not bring in those dumbass boys to drive her price up and make me crazy?"

A little wicked grin flashed on the artist's face before he became serious again. "I have no idea what you're talking about."

"You know exactly what I'm talking about. Did you bring those boys to town to ogle my wife and milk me for cash? They were talking about my sister, you know."

Stef held his hands out as though to placate the beast he found himself with. Rachel thought he should have brought out a chair and maybe a whip. "I would never let Bay and Shane anywhere near Brooke. Brooke would eat them alive, and Bay is too talented an artist to die. Seriously, I've just started collecting him. His stuff is going to be worth millions one day. I don't want Brooke to screw that up."

"Shit. He shouldn't have done that." Rye sighed like the outcome was now inevitable. Rachel felt his hands wrap around her waist.

Max practically vibrated with rage. "Asshole! That's exactly what you did. I bet you gave them the cash they bid with. Those cowboys couldn't afford two grand."

Stefan gave it up and began laughing loudly. "That asshole cowboy is who the grant is for. He's a sculptor. He applied for the Foundation grant this year. You paid three thousand dollars for a woman who already wanted you, and one of the guys you were trying to keep her away from is getting the money."

Rye pulled her away from the window. Rachel found herself flat on her back, legs spread, with Rye's face nuzzling her neck. "They'll be at it for a while, baby. We'll have to find something to occupy our time while they beat each other down."

"I'm gonna kill you this time, Stef!"

Rachel tried to get up, but Rye held her down. "Don't you think we should stop that?" Rachel asked.

"Hey! Not my hands," Stefan was screaming back at Max. "Or my face!" There was a loud groan as someone got smacked.

Rye seemed blissfully unconcerned. "Nah. They do this at least once a year. I think they both have an inner need to kick some ass, and this way no one really gets hurt. I mean, at least Max doesn't get hurt. Usually." Rye continued kissing her neck as his hard cock found her pussy. He entered her with one long thrust.

Rachel gasped and locked her legs around Rye's waist. He thrust in and out easily, as though he enjoyed the exercise.

His face was serene as he gazed down at her. "I think a psychiatrist would say Stef has some deep-seated issues that cause him to seek out pain. Max is really just therapy for him. About once a year, he pulls something that causes Max to beat the shit out of him. The next day, Max has to buy the beer, and we all go back to being friends."

"That's terrible." She managed to breathe through the pounding of her heart. Rye was slowly grinding against her clit. He knew exactly how to play her.

He shrugged and continued fucking her. "That's just Max." She could see he was still looking out the small window over the bed. He grimaced. "And that's a black eye. Sorry, Stef got in a lucky shot."

Rachel was about to ask if Max was all right when Rye exerted just the right amount of pressure. The orgasm caught her off guard. She gasped as her body seized and released in spasms of pleasure. Through it all, she could see Rye looking incredibly pleased with himself. She had the feeling he could go on for hours, but the door to the cabin slammed open, and he grimaced.

"Time's almost up. Next time you come five times before I let go." Rye picked up the pace. Within a minute she felt the wash of his release as Max slammed into the room.

Rye rolled off her. He was every inch the satisfied man. His eyes were lazy as he looked at his brother. "What did you force him into this time?"

Max was sporting a hell of a cut over his right eye. Rachel sat up and tried to look at it. "He's paying for our honeymoon. So, baby, you pick someplace expensive. We're going first-class all the way. That should teach him to mess with me." Max reached down and scooped her up into his arms before she could protest. He glared at Rye. "And you. She's probably sore. Do you give her any time at all to recoup from our sexual marathon? Hell no, you're on top of her the minute you wake up."

Rye grinned. He was devastating when he smiled. "Not the minute. We watched you yell at Stef for a while."

"I'm going to take her to bathe," Max said, sounding as prim as a half-naked man with a black eye could sound. "Maybe she'll feel better after a nice long soak."

He started to carry her off when Rye laughed. "Baby, you do know he's going to fuck you in the tub, don't you?"

Max's hungry smile told her everything she needed to know.

Thirty minutes later, the water was still warm as Rye eased into the marble monstrosity of a tub. Max moved back a little, making room for his brother to sit opposite them. His arms were lazily wrapped around Rachel. She let her head fall back against his chest. She was going to take a long nap when they got home. Rye pulled her feet into his hands and started rubbing.

"That feels good." Rachel sighed.

"I'm glad to help," Rye replied with a wink. "Tell me, baby, did he even let you get into the tub, or did he just bend you over the sink?"

Max's head came up. "Hey, I was a gentleman. I shoved her up against the wall. I did all the work. All she had to do was hold on."

"Yes, it was all very polite." Rachel reached down in the warm water and found Max's hand. She wound her fingers through his. "Listen, Max, I never meant for the bidding to get crazy like that. I have some money…"

Max nibbled on her ear. "It's fine, Rach. Don't worry about it. I'm pissed at Stef, not you. I can't be mad at you for bringing us together."

She shivered as Max sucked on her sensitive earlobe. "No, I want to put in my share. I have about seven hundred dollars. I know it's not much."

"We'll take it," Rye announced, never letting up on his slow rub. His strong hands worked the arches of her feet. She would have given him every cent just for him to continue.

"Rye, she is not paying us back."

Rye shrugged. "All right. I just thought, that since we were getting married, we should probably set up a household account and put all the money in it. If you think Rachel should have a separate account..."

"Hell no!" Max turned her around so he could see her face. Rachel protested the loss of her foot massage, but Max didn't seem to care. "Let's get one thing straight, Rachel. This is not one of those roommate-style marriages where we just come together for sex. This is a traditional family. We make the decisions together, and everything we have is ours."

Rachel suppressed her need to laugh. "Yes, I can plainly see how traditional we are," she remarked to the man she planned on referring to as Husband Number One.

Husband Number Two smiled brightly. "Maybe we should change the name of the business to the Harper-Swift Stables. I don't want Rachel to feel left out."

A vein right above Max's left eye throbbed and looked as though it might explode. "Why the hell would you keep your name? You're marrying us, Rachel. You'll take our name. Even if this marriage is a damn democracy, we can outvote you. You're going to be Mrs. Harper."

Rachel stared at Husband Number Two. "Will you stop baiting him?"

"But it's fun."

She shook her head. "Stop it." She turned to Max. "You calm down, you Neanderthal. I never said I wanted a separate account, and I never wanted to keep my last name." She bit her bottom lip, gnawing at it nervously. Now was as good a time as any to fess up. It was time they knew about her past. Rachel was surprised to find she wasn't terribly worried about how they would react. Something soft, but infinitely strong, settled into her heart. They loved her. They would never leave her. It gave her enormous security. She reached out and took both their hands in hers. "The truth is, I'm not that attached to this name."

She felt both of them tense.

"How attached are you to Elizabeth Courtney?" Rye asked quietly.

She felt her eyes widen and her mouth drop open. "You know?"

Max nodded. "Yeah, baby. I searched your car and found your fake IDs."

"You searched my car?"

Max didn't even bother to look guilty. He simply nodded. "Oh, yeah. I would have searched your house, if you had one."

"He's a nosy guy," Rye interjected.

"Well, you were obviously hiding something." Max's fingers curled around hers.

"And it never occurred to you to give me my privacy?" Rachel know the answer but felt compelled to ask any way.

"Nope," Max replied.

Rye joined him. "No, darlin'. And just to fess up, I would have searched your car, but Max got there first. You know, I did run a trace on you."

Her heart raced a little. She had tried not to think about the fact that Rye had requested information on her. Tommy still had contacts in the police departments all across the southwest.

Rye's face was set in stern lines as he sat back against the curved wall of the tub. He did not look like a man who was going to let her go because he was shocked at the truth. "You were running. No one shows up in Bliss with just the clothes on their back and a beat-up Jeep as a living space."

Max immediately refuted his brother's statement. "Now, the way Mom told it, that was pretty much the way Teeny showed up. And

Holly Lang, you know, that waitress at the Bear Creek Lounge. Oh, and don't forget Laura Niles. She's the checkout girl at the Stop 'n' Shop. She didn't even have a car, though. She hitchhiked into town and liked it so much she stayed."

Rye's feet rubbed against hers under the warm, bubbly water. "Teeny was living in her VW bus with Logan, and she was on the run from an abusive husband. Marie took care of him with her twelve-gauge."

"There is a reason I play it safe about Marie. That old woman can still castrate a man at twenty paces," Max murmured.

"Can we skip the roundtable discussion of women on the run?" Rachel interrupted. If she let them go on, she would hear about every woman who ever sought refuge in Bliss, and it seemed like there were a whole lot of them. Maybe they should form a club. "So you know about Tommy?"

Rye and Max got very serious. "Yes, I know all about him," Rye replied. "I'm going to make sure he can't hurt you again. I think we should all go back to Dallas on Monday. We'll stand beside you while you press charges."

She took a deep, steadying breath. She had been pretty sure that was what she needed to do. She didn't want to hide for the rest of her life. How could she move on, marry Max and Rye, and have babies with them if she was always looking over her shoulder? Her running days were over. She'd only run in the first place because she'd been all alone. She wasn't alone anymore. She had more than just her life to fight for. She was fighting for a future.

"I'm ready." She squeezed their hands.

Rye pulled her close. "I love you. He'll have to kill me to get to you."

"And while he's killing Rye, we'll run, Rach," Max promised with a glimmer in his eye.

Rye groaned and splashed his brother in the face.

Rachel tried to get out of the line of fire. In the end, she gave in and splashed them both. She was going home to face her demons, but she wasn't going alone.

# Chapter Sixteen

The sun was high in the sky as Rye drove them home. They chatted about their upcoming trip to Texas. It made her nervous, but she decided she would view it as a vacation. She would put things right so she could get on with her life. Rye was going to book the trip when they got home. Rachel was going to pack what little she had. The men promised to take her shopping while they were in Dallas. She wasn't going to live out of her car anymore, and they had a huge closet for her to fill up. Rye promised they would shop for wedding rings while they were in the big city.

She would need some winter clothes. She bet it got cold here. She'd never lived in a place where it snowed all winter long. It wouldn't matter. She had two heat generators to keep her warm in bed. She'd been cozy cuddled between them the night before.

Rye turned down the long drive that led to the house. She was getting used to the quiet of the ranch. It was isolated, with only two neighbors and the nudist colony within a five mile radius.

Rye leaned forward and peered in the distance. "What is that?"

Max rolled down the back window. He breathed deeply. "It's smoke."

She smelled the woody smell of smoke billowing in through the window. A cold shiver went through Rachel's body as she remembered that night when Tommy tried to kill her. She had woken to the overwhelming smell of smoke. It had choked her and caused her to gag. She'd been forced to crawl on her belly to find even the smallest patch of breathable air.

"If those idiot boys set off one of their rockets again, I'm going to have a long talk with their mama," Max swore. "I told them to keep those fire hazards on their own property."

Rye reached for her and squeezed her hand. "It's fine, Rachel. Max is probably right. Those Farley boys more than likely have another wild science project going. They're ambitious, but not the brightest bulbs in the socket, if you know what I mean. They live on the other side of the valley. More often than not, though, they end up in our pasture. If it's not them, then someone is ignoring the burn ban, and I'm going to get to write a ticket or two."

Rachel nodded, but she gripped Rye's hand. She hated the smell of smoke. It put her right back in that night when she'd fought for her life. She remembered the moment when she realized she couldn't leave the bedroom. The doorknob had been hot to the touch. The fire had spread, and there was only one way out of her small townhouse. She'd been forced to break the window and jump. She could still feel the glass cutting her flesh and the terror of hitting the ground. She'd been sure Tommy would be waiting to do what his fire hadn't been able to. Only the sounds of her neighbors coming out of their homes to check out what was happening had driven him off, she was sure of it. Even then, she had been able to feel his eyes on her, watching her. She shook off the feeling now. She wouldn't let him ruin every good moment she had.

"Hey." Max reached for her from his seat in the back. He seemed to sense her fear. His hands were a comfort around her shoulders. "Are you all right, baby?"

She took a deep breath and tried to banish the panic. "I'm fine." She was all right. She was with them. There was no way Tommy had caught up to her. She'd been very careful since he'd almost caught her in San Diego. It was just the fire that was making her edgy. She just had to stay calm. It wouldn't do to have her future husbands see her flip out at the very smell of smoke.

Rye pulled up to the house. The smoke seemed thicker than before. It bloomed from behind the house, a gray-and-white cloud growing by the minute.

Max was out of the car in a shot. His face was ashen as he realized what was on fire. "It's the stables," he said with an air of disbelief.

Rachel knew those horses meant the world to Max. He'd worked so hard to build his business, and now it was on fire.

"Damn it. I have to go and get the horses out." He looked at Rye, and his blue eyes stark. "Why don't you get her out of here? Take her back to Stefan's. He's got a security system. Call the fire department on the way."

Rachel scrambled out of the Bronco. "No, I'm going with you. I can help." There was no way she was leaving him here to fight a fire and rescue the horses alone. Bliss only had a volunteer fire company. She had no idea how that worked, but she knew Max wouldn't wait for them. He'd do everything he could to save the stables.

She watched as Max and Rye passed a wary glance between them. Rye reached into the back of the Bronco. He pulled out a shotgun and extra ammunition. After making sure it was loaded, he passed it off to Max. Max slipped the extra ammo in his pocket.

Rye nodded to his brother. "Go check it out. I'll call in the fire over the radio. If I need to, I'll get her out of here, but I'd rather stay and help you."

"All right," Max replied tightly. His face was a mask of tension as he looked her over and then spoke to his brother. "If I can get the horses out safely, I'm going to. You take care of our girl."

He gave her a long look before turning and heading out. Max held the shotgun with the ease of a man who knew how to use it. He jogged off toward the stables, where the smoke was billowing into the air.

"Why can't we go with him?" Rachel held on to Rye's sleeve like it was a lifeline.

Rye hugged her for a moment and then gently disentangled himself. He moved back to the driver's side of the car. Rye leaned into the Bronco and pulled out the radio. "I have to keep you safe, Rachel. This doesn't feel right. Stay close to me." He pushed the button to talk. "Callie, this is Rye. Are you there?"

Callie's voice was tinny over the radio. "That's an affirmative, boss." Rachel turned away from Rye. She tried to catch a glimpse of Max in the distance. He'd disappeared from sight.

"I need you to call the fire truck out to our place."

Rye's voice was calm as she struggled to see how bad the fire was. Her feet itched to run down there so Max wouldn't be alone.

"And send Logan down here, too. Pull him off of whatever he's doing. Tell him to bring a couple of extra shotguns with him. Callie, I need you to put out the word—" Rye's voice died as Rachel heard a hard *thwack*.

"Rye, are you there?" Callie's voice spiked with obvious worry.

Rachel turned in time to watch Rye slide, unconscious, to the ground. The handset of the radio swung uselessly against the side of the SUV. She could see he was bleeding. Her heart started to pound. There was so much blood.

"Hello, Liz."

Rachel's stomach churned as she saw her nightmare standing over Rye. He had a baseball bat in his hand.

Tommy Lane stood roughly six feet tall. He was all rangy muscle. His face was a testament to hard living, and there was always cruelty in his eyes. He had always reminded Rachel a little of a rodent, since his eyes were too small for his face. They were black and often seemed to have no emotion behind them. That was not the case now. He stood looking her over with a stark possessiveness that made her skin crawl.

It didn't matter, Rachel thought, her mind racing. All that mattered was saving Rye. God, he couldn't already be dead. He was still bleeding on the ground. The grass around him was becoming saturated. She started to move toward him, but Tommy dropped the bat and pulled a handgun out of the holster he wore.

"Don't you touch him." Tommy's voice was low and ragged. "You lay a hand on him, and I'll put a bullet through his brain."

Rachel stopped. She knew he would do just what he'd threatened. She was surprised to see Quigley wander up. The big dog whined a little as he sniffed at Rye's body. He licked Rye's face and tried to get him to wake up. Rye was completely still.

Tommy laughed as the dog tried to wake his master. "Dumb dog. I thought I'd have to shoot that monster when I got out here to set up that little distraction in the stables. The stupid dog just wanted to play. I threw a stick for him a couple of times, and now he's my best friend. Those boys of yours need better security."

"Please don't hurt him again." Rachel concentrated only on the fact that Rye might be dying. She tried to keep her voice calm. She didn't want to make Tommy any angrier than he already was. She wanted to run, to get away from here. He was going to kill her, and she doubted it would be a quick death. He would want some revenge on her for running. Her feet remained firmly planted. She couldn't abandon Rye. If she had a chance to save her men, then she had to take it. They hadn't done anything wrong except to have the misfortune to fall for her. "I'll go with you if you leave them alone."

Tommy's mouth turned up in a ghoulish version of a smile. "You'll come with me, Liz. You'll come with me because you're mine, and I don't let go of what belongs to me. You should have learned that by now. My truck is over the ridge, off the road. We're going to walk to it, and then we'll go someplace where we can talk."

She shivered. She knew there wouldn't be a lot of talking. There would probably be a brutal rape followed by him gutting her. She wasn't an idiot, but Rye's still body caused her to agree. She thought she saw his chest moving. She prayed he was still breathing. She couldn't take the chance that Tommy would finish him off. Max could be back any minute. He would be walking into a trap, and

Tommy was a trained professional. Rachel doubted he would hesitate to shoot Max. After all, she realized, he had already shot him.

"You've been here for two weeks," Rachel said. He'd been the one behind Max getting shot, not some hunters.

His arrogant smile was all the answer she needed, but he responded anyway. "I've been watching you, Liz. I almost took out your boyfriend. That horse of his bucked, and I missed my shot. I thought the horse would do him in when it panicked, but he must have a hard head. Of course, I had no idea you had the other one on your string, too." He kicked at Rye's body.

"Stop, please," she practically begged as Rye's body slumped back down. Quigley whined and came to sit at her feet.

Tommy pointed the gun at Rye's head. For a moment she thought he was going to shoot. "Tell me, Liz, how does it feel to whore yourself out to two men? What kind of woman does that? Did you think I would let you get away with it?"

"No." She would tell him anything if it got him to move that gun away from Rye's head.

He pointed the gun at her and took a deep breath. "You walk in front of me. I hear one scream out of you, and I shoot him and that other fucker, you understand?"

She nodded and started to walk. Tommy pointed to the woods they'd just driven through. She started up the steep climb. It led back to the road she'd nearly driven off of earlier in the week.

"How did you find me?" Rachel asked quietly as she climbed. Quigley panted beside her. She wished that Max and Rye had trained the big, dumb dog to kill. Here was an animal of mammoth proportions, which should have been a vicious predator, and instead he ambled along beside her, probably hoping for a treat.

"I found you because I'm smarter than you, Liz," Tommy rasped. She could hear he was already struggling with the altitude. They were going up a slow, steady incline. Tommy was in shape, but he came from a place that was barely above sea level. Rachel had weeks of acclimation on him. They were still too close to the house, she thought as they walked into the woods. When they got farther up, she would run. She had no intention of docilely getting into his truck. If he wanted to kill her, he was going to have to work for it.

"That backhills sheriff you've been fucking called around looking for information on one Rachel Swift," Tommy explained. "Stupid. I figured out you had help a long time ago. I traced a line from that nosy, interfering nurse to a man named Lonnie Hayes. He's a two-striker, Liz. He helps out the nurse, but his main business is fake IDs for kids and people who want to disappear. I leaned on him. He spat out your fake names faster than my fists worked. No one wants to go to jail. Those high-and-mighty principles go straight out the door when a person is faced with hard time."

Rachel's heart was pounding. She thought about all the people who helped her along the way. What kind of danger had she placed them in? "Did you kill him?"

Tommy laughed. "No, but he didn't work for a while. It's hard to type when your hands are broken. I did kill old Auntie Sadie, though."

Rachel stopped and turned. She had a sudden vision of her sweet, elderly aunt. She'd been so kind to her as a child. "You killed my aunt?"

Tommy shrugged. "I knew you would come see her one last time. You couldn't help yourself. She was on her way out anyway. I just gave her a shove in the right direction."

Rachel's hands started to shake, and it was with a righteous anger. That anger was blocking out fear and all of her survival instincts. This man had taken everything from her. He'd terrified her and made her life miserable. He'd driven away her friends and killed her dog. She'd lost her job and her aunt and her home to him. And why? Because she wouldn't go on a second date with him? Because she wouldn't cede her body to him and take his abuse?

"You bastard," she said, not recognizing the growl that came from her throat. It was a predatory growl, not the sound of a prey animal.

"You watch your tongue with me, girl," Tommy said. His every word dripped with threat.

"How dare you?" Rachel snarled. "You pathetic piece of shit. Do you have any idea the hell you've put me through?"

"No less than you've put me through, Liz." His dark eyes were glassy. "You women think you can take and take from a man and never have to give back."

"I didn't take anything from you!" Rachel screamed. "You are delusional if you think for one second that we had any kind of a relationship."

"I loved you!" Tommy didn't seem to care now that his voice resounded through the trees. "You treated me like shit, and I won't take it. I don't take that from any woman."

She was through, she realized with a shock. She was through running, and she was through taking his crap. With a rage she hadn't known herself capable of, she launched herself at him.

His eyes widened as she threw her body at him. It seemed to take him off guard, and his hand flew back. Rachel heard the gun go off as it hit the ground yards away. Quigley barked and ran away. It didn't matter. All that mattered was showing Tommy Lane that she wasn't his victim anymore. Rachel let herself go. She screamed and scratched at him. She used her nails on his face and tried to get at his eyes. She was satisfied with his groan as she planted her knee in his belly when he fell back to the ground.

It didn't take him long to recover. After a moment of trying to guard his face, Tommy shoved at her with his strong arms. He pushed against her chest, and she flew back. She hit the ground and tried to scramble up. It was too late. He was fast. He was on his feet in an instant, hauling her up by her hair.

"You think I need that gun, Liz?" He spat the question in her ear. She gritted her teeth against the pain in her scalp. He pulled her close. They were chest to chest. "I was never going to use that gun on you. It's too fast. It wouldn't teach you the lesson you need to learn."

His mouth was pressed to her ear. She struggled, but he held her firmly.

"I brought this for you, Liz," he whispered as though he'd brought her flowers he wanted her to admire.

Rachel swallowed as he pulled out a wicked-looking knife. The silver knife glittered in the sunlight. It was long, and there was no question what it was used for. Some knives had a utilitarian purpose. This knife had been made to kill.

"It's for you, Liz. I made it special, and I'll bury it with you."

He started to pull the knife back. Rachel knew she had mere seconds before he shoved it into her belly. She brought her knee up as hard as she could and aimed directly for his testicles. He groaned as she made rough contact. His hand let go of her hair. She stumbled backward.

"You bitch!" Tommy screamed as he cupped himself.

Rachel didn't think. She turned and ran. She felt Quigley running beside her, but she couldn't afford to look down. She just ran, knowing Tommy was behind her every step of the way. If she could just make it to the road, she knew Mel's house was right across the way. She would start screaming. If she had any luck at all, he would hear her and come running.

Tears streamed down her face as she ran. Branches and shrubs cut into her. She ignored them. Her lungs burned. Still she ran. She could hear him catching up.

"I'm going to make you scream, bitch!"

She moved to the left. She could see the road come into view. She was almost there. Then she was falling. She hit the ground hard. The breath was knocked from her lungs as she slammed down. Her ankle twisted painfully.

She forced herself to turn over and tried to get up, but she'd tripped on a rock. Her ankle was swelling before her eyes. Her heart seized. They would find her here. Max and Rye—*please let him be alive*—they would find her body here. They would be so heartbroken. She would give anything for just one more minute with them.

"Poor Liz," Tommy said, walking slowly toward her. The knife was in his hand. He looked satisfied that she couldn't run anymore. It was apparent from the light in his eyes that he wanted to play with her.

Quigley nudged her with his nose, and Rachel realized he had something in his mouth. He dropped it on her lap. Quigley had gone after the gun. Someone had thrown it, so in his doggy mind, it was something to be fetched. His huge mouth had easily carried the handgun.

Without hesitation, Rachel picked up the gun and fired. There was no warning. He had given her none. There was no request to stop or she would shoot. There was not even the inkling in her mind that now she could send him to jail. There was only the need to be free of him once and for all. Rachel pulled the trigger again.

He looked down at the expanding red blossom on his chest. His eyes registered a dull sort of shock. He staggered toward her, still holding the knife as though he would take her with him.

Rachel pulled the trigger yet again.

He stopped at the third shot, and his knees buckled. He fell face-first to the ground.

"Rachel!" She could hear Max screaming for her.

She got to her feet. Her ankle protested, but she had to get up. Her whole body shook. She felt tears streaming down her face. Blood pounded through her body reminding her that she was alive. She was alive. She had won. She stood over Tommy Lane, and it wasn't enough. She aimed at his head. Rachel pulled the trigger one last time to be sure.

"Rachel!" Max's tormented scream reverberated through the woods.

Quigley barked. His tail thumped, and he took off looking for his master.

Rachel was still holding the gun when Max burst into view following Quigley. He was running full out, shotgun firmly in his hand. He stopped when he saw the scene before him.

"Oh God, baby," he breathed, walking to her.

She dropped the gun and fell into him, sobbing the whole time. Max's arms tightened around her until she thought she might burst. His hands ran over her body, looking for damage.

"You did good, baby. You did so good. I'm so sorry I wasn't here." He pulled her close and kissed her forehead.

Rachel felt his tears on her shoulder. She looked up. Panic seized her again. "Rye?"

"Is a lot slower since someone used his skull for batting practice." The words were low, but the sight of Rye walking toward her with a shirt wrapped around his head was the most beautiful thing she'd ever seen. She limped over to him, holding on to Max and gently kissed Rye. His face was tight with pain, but he held on to her as though she was the fragile one.

"You need to go to the hospital." Rachel wouldn't be satisfied until he'd had every test known to the medical world.

"They're on their way." Max pressed himself against her back as Rye hugged her front. She sent a silent prayer of thanks to anyone listening.

In the distance, she heard the sound of the ambulance making its way up the road.

She looked down at Tommy's body. He didn't matter anymore. She was in their arms, wrapped in her future, and no one could take that away from her.

# Epilogue

Rachel watched her husband toss the drool-covered tennis ball into the yard. Quigley wagged his stubby tail and happily ran off after it.

"You're going to throw your arm out." She sank down into the rocking chair beside him. He'd been playing fetch for hours with the dog.

Max smiled at her. "It's little enough payment for what he did." He reached over and grabbed her hand. He did that a lot, she'd noticed. He held her hand whenever they sat together.

It had been a month since that day in the woods. Rachel had cherished every day with them. She looked down at the ring on her finger. It was a solitaire that had been their mother's, and it was surrounded by two small golden bands.

Rachel had married Max in a small courthouse, but she would never really consider that her wedding. That had been a thing to appease legalities. Her real wedding day had been one week ago. The entire town of Bliss had gathered as she stood in front of their family and friends and pledged to love Max and Rye for the rest of her life. It was the easiest promise she'd ever made.

She'd made one more legal change. She was legally Rachel Elizabeth Harper. Somehow she couldn't go back to her old name. It didn't fit her anymore. She was a new person.

"Rye's home." Max pointed to the brand new truck coming up the road.

Rye parked, gave Quigley a pat, and threw the tennis ball. He smiled broadly as he stepped onto the porch.

"I am officially a free man," he said before he leaned over to kiss her.

"How does it feel not to be Johnny Law anymore, brother?" Max asked.

Rachel knew how happy Max was that Rye was coming back to work at the stables. They had spent weeks planning the new services they could offer. They were offering riding lessons now that Rye had the time to teach. Rachel had the feeling a lot of ladies would sign up for Rye to teach them how to ride. She would have to be patient.

Rye took the chair on her right side. "It feels good. No more dealing with tourists, or placating Mel, or being worried about having to toss my own brother in jail."

"Yeah, now you can be my alibi in good conscience," Max replied.

"I met the new sheriff." Rye rocked back and forth. It was how they ended their days, together, watching the sunset. "I thought Callie's eyes were going to pop out of her head."

"Good-looking?" Rachel made a mental note to call Callie and get the lowdown on the new Sheriff.

"His name is Nathan Wright. He used to work for the DEA or something like it. Callie seemed really surprised to see him. I think she's met him somewhere. I suppose he's okay, if you like the type."

Max frowned. "She doesn't. Rachel likes our type."

"Yes, I do. I just hope he's a hottie who shakes up Callie's world. I can't be the only love slave in Bliss."

"Oh, baby, you won't be. Not as long as Stef has a pulse. Now," Rye said with a sly look in his eyes, "I can concentrate on teaching one very special girl how to ride. I start Rachel's lessons tomorrow."

Rachel felt a secret smile curl on her lips.

"Hell, Rye, I'll start teaching her how to ride tonight." Max leered at her happily.

"I meant on a horse, idiot," Rye joked with affection. "She's going to run the business part of this, but she needs to know how to ride properly. You said that mare we picked out for her should be here in the morning."

"I think I might wait a while for those lessons, Rye." Her hand went over her still-flat stomach.

"Hey, there's nothing to be afraid of, Rach." He looked slightly concerned. "I'm a good teacher. I won't yell at you like Max would."

Max opened his mouth and then shut it. He nodded shortly, conceding the point.

"It's not that," Rachel explained. "I just don't think it would be good for the baby."

There was a long pause.

"Rachel?" Max stopped rocking.

"Are you sure?" Rye's face was a mask of stunned expectation.

"I'm as sure as three pregnancy tests can be," she replied with a grin. "I wanted to tell you fast because I bought them at the Stop 'n' Shop, so everyone knows by now."

Max was on his knees, his big hand covering her belly. "I can't believe it."

"I can," Rye said, grinning from ear to ear. "We've tried hard enough."

Then they were off. They argued about names and whether it would be a boy or a girl. They decided which room to convert to a nursery and where he or she would be going to college.

Rachel sat back and rocked as they planned the future. Her hand rested contentedly on the small life growing inside her. All around her, the world seemed safe and lovely. She watched as the sun went down and night fell softly on Bliss.

# THE END

**www.sophieoak.com**

# ABOUT THE AUTHOR

A lifetime devotee to the written word, Sophie published her first novel, *Small Town Siren* this year. Prior to becoming a novelist, she worked in theater and comic books. She lives in Fort Worth, Texas with her husband and three precocious children, who wonder when mom is going to write a book they will be allowed to read. Her answer: probably never. Sophie believes in happy endings for everyone, no matter how extreme the story. Her stories may feature some of the fringe elements of sexuality, but at heart they are always about love. *Small Town Siren, Siren in the City,* and *Three to Ride (Nights in Bliss 1)* are available now. Please feel free to contact her at sophie@sophieoak.com.

## *Also by Sophie Oak*

Ménage Amour: Texas Sirens 1: *Small Town Siren*
Ménage Amour: Texas Sirens 2: *Siren in the City*
Siren Classic: *Away From Me*
Ménage Everlasting: Nights in Bliss, Colorado 2*: Two to Love*


Available at
**BOOKSTRAND.COM**

**Siren Publishing, Inc.**
**www.SirenPublishing.com**

Breinigsville, PA USA
09 February 2011
255179BV00006B/55/P